Praise for *Ginger Mancino, Kid Comedian*

"Funny, heartwarming and adorable! Ginger's story will resonate with funny kids everywhere."

—Jenny Lawson, author of #1 New York Times bestsellers
Furiously Happy and *Let's Pretend This Never Happened*

"I sure could have used a book like Kid Comedian when I was a pre-teen. Ginger Mancino is funny and real, and the timelessness of her emotions makes them relatable to anyone who has ever attended middle school. While Ginger is smart, funny and curious, sometimes things do not go her way. Reading along as she discovers the importance of developing positive relationships, and the strength to persist after making mistakes offers readers the chance to emerge a little better, a little wiser. Wendi Aarons writes with respect for young readers and a deep understanding that we fumble and triumph as we discover ourselves."

—Meredith Walker, co-founder and executive director
of Amy Poehler's Smart Girls

"Equal parts witty and awkweird, Ginger Mancino is a comic hero for the ages—provided she can survive middle school. A funny, joyful story that provides a laugh and a heart tug on every page."

—Shari Simpson, author of *Sam Saves the Night* and
the upcoming Disney Books series, *The Sugar Rush Racers*

"A hilarious and deeply touching story for anyone who has ever felt different. Ginger Mancino is a tenacious force and reminds us all that you don't have to conform to shine your light. Ginger Mancino, Kid Comedian is a legit hit!"

—Melissa Savage, author of *Lemons* and *Karma Moon—Ghost Hunter*

"Comedy is hard, but so is growing up. Ginger's determination to master both makes for a compelling, heartfelt, and hilarious read!"

—Jennifer Ziegler, author of *The Brewster Triplets series* and *Worser*

"Ginger's hilarious comedy routines, self-deprecating candor, and generous heart left me convulsed in giggles but also enriched by the genuine wisdom to be found in the search for laughter."

—Claudia Mills, author of *The Lost Language and Write This Down*

Ginger Mancino,
KID COMEDIAN

BY WENDI AARONS

Paperback 978-1-7339887-4-2
Ebook 978-1-7339887-5-9

First paperback edition: June 2022

Cover art and book design by Basia Tran

Printed by BookBar Press in the USA

bookbar**press**

BookBar Press
4280 Tennyson Street
Denver, Colorado 80212
www.bookbarpress.com

FOR EVERY FUNNY KID OUT THERE,
AND THE PEOPLE WHO LOVE THEM.

CHAPTER ONE

I was twelve when I experienced the worst moment of my life. Right before "the moment," I was in my happy place. I stood in the wings of a comedy club stage with a bottle of water in one hand and a piece of notebook paper in the other. At the top of the paper, the word JOKES was written in purple ink, with a few loopy sentences scrawled beneath it.

If you'd seen me that night, I probably would've looked like another boring kid. Medium height, medium brown hair, medium pale skin, medium braces, but I was far from boring. I knew more about comedy and making people laugh than anyone else my age.

If you'd seen me that night, you would have noticed how I watched the comedian on stage in front of me with a laser-like intensity. He was getting huge laughs and applause from the audience with his rants about airline peanuts and his wife's shopping addiction. I chuckled softly at his jokes, but I was studying him more than enjoying his act. Almost like it was my job or something. Because it was.

It was at this point in the night that my ears perked up as voices emerged in the dark hallway behind me.

"Who's on after Billy?"

"Let me check . . . oh. It's your client, Ginger Mancino. The kid comedian."

I turned slightly at the sound of my name. The comedy club owner and my talent manager were chatting by a stack of chairs. I wanted to call out to them, wave "Hi," but I had to stay quiet. There was a show going on. I'd been in shows a million times, after all, and I knew the proper behavior. It definitely wasn't my first rodeo. Instead, I looked down at the page of jokes in my hand and bounced up and down on my heels, full of nervous excitement to soon be in the spotlight. Oh, how I loved being in the spotlight.

Then I overheard something that changed my life forever.

"Is it just me, or is Ginger's act not exactly cute anymore? I think our kid comedian has entered an awkward phase."

My mouth dropped open. My head felt dizzy. Did I hear that right? How could the club owner say such an awful thing about me? Awkward? Not cute? Me? My act? My stomach churned with upset butterflies. I waited for my manager, who had booked me in shows for years and had lovingly guided my career like a parent, to come to my defense. Instead she just groaned.

"Ugh, I know. No audience wants to look at a gawky preteen telling school lunch jokes that are more suited to an eight-year-old. It's depressing. She doesn't know it yet, but I'm dropping her from my roster right after tonight's show."

Angry, embarrassed tears filled my eyes, and I

quickly blinked to stop the waterworks. I shakily took a sip from my water bottle then looked around to make sure nobody saw how humiliated I felt. I was devastated. Wrecked. I felt wobbly, like I'd just crashed into a brick wall. Comedy was my life. It was all I knew. But before a single teardrop had a chance to slide down my cheek, before I could even process the shock that this may be my last time on stage as a comic, the wacky emcee of the show glanced over at me, nodded, then boomed into the mic, "Now, put your hands together for Ginger Mancino, the kid comedian!"

And that was it. My worst moment. I would soon be boring in every and all ways. I would no longer be special. But that night, I had no other choice but to force a big, cheesy smile and bound into the spotlight midstage, hoping I could make people laugh while I tried as hard as I could to not bawl like a baby. I was a professional comedian, after all.

Now I'm not so sure who I am.

CHAPTER TWO

"Take a seat, Ginger." Mrs. G sits behind her big brown desk. The top of the desk is covered in messy piles of papers and folders plus a Torchy's taco she plans to eat for lunch. It smells delicious, and I'm just about to ask if I can have a bite when she says, "Let's talk about what happened yesterday."

I wish I could tell you that Mrs. G is a powerful talent agent who has exciting news for me about my career, but unfortunately, she's not. She's my guidance counselor at Davy Crockett Middle School in Austin, Texas, where I am currently (unsuccessfully) trying to survive the seventh grade. The soundtrack of my life used to be applause. Now it's just a sad trombone. *Wut wahhhhhhhh.*

I've spent a lot of time in Mrs. G's office since I started school a few months ago, and we've grown close. Or as close as a twelve-year-old girl who doesn't have a single friend and a grouchy middle-aged administrator who drives a dented minivan named Thor can be. Which is to say, not very.

I plop down in her surprisingly comfortable yellow guest chair, the one I've heard classmates call "the hot seat," but unlike them, it doesn't make me feel like I'm in trouble. It makes me feel like I'm on the talk show circuit as a kid comedian again. Before I realize it, I'm telling Mrs. G an amusing anecdote. "Jimmy Kimmel helped me with my math homework once." I lean toward her with a grin. "When I was a guest on his talk show. Then, when my tutor graded the paper, I got an F! Jimmy should stick to comedy, am I right?"

I sit back and wait for her to laugh, but all Mrs. G gives me is a heavy sigh and a few clicks of the black pen in her hand. Nothing like bombing at 2 p.m. on a Tuesday!

Deflated, I return her sigh. "Listen, Mrs. G, I haven't been on the school PA system ever since you canceled my *G'Day with Ginger* show two months ago because apparently nobody liked hearing my voice at 8 a.m. And I'm no longer heckling my teachers while they teach. Also, I've stopped sitting down uninvited with different groups of kids in the cafeteria and offering to tell them jokes in exchange for fish sticks. I realize now that's creepy. I'm behaving. I promise! I'm doing everything you told me to—wait, is this because of what happened at lunch yesterday? Because that totally wasn't my fault."

It totally was my fault.

The incident in question happened when Mrs. Paulson, the lunchroom monitor who wears muscle shirts and Crocs, earning her the nickname "The Cafeteria Crocodile Hunter," left her microphone unattended when she went to pull some string cheese out of a sixth grader's nose. (The school monitors use microphones to tell us when to get seconds or when

7

it's time to leave because there are a ton of kids in the lunchroom. The whole dining experience is like *The Hunger Games* every single day, but with tater tots!) I happened to notice the live mic sitting there on the table and, well, *Hello, gorgeous*. I love microphones more than Lady Gaga loves putting glitter on a squirrel and wearing it as a winter hat. I practically grew up with a mic in my hand.

"Yes, Ginger, what happened at lunch yesterday is exactly why you're here. I've received a lot of complaints from parents who didn't appreciate their children being subjected to—what was it you called your little act?"

"The Middle School Mystery Meat Show," I mumble. "Where's the Beef?"

"Yes, that. Your joke about cows eating lunch in the CALFeteria was, frankly, not funny. But when you yelled that your burger was still 'moo-ving,' you really caused a disturbance. Two students were so upset they couldn't even finish their lunches."

"Maybe they'll be vegans now. That's not a bad thing!" I try, but she doesn't budge. "Well, I thought my routine was funny." I look down at my lap and wonder for the millionth time why I'm the only person at this school who ever laughs at my jokes.

"Ginger." Mrs. G exhales, staring at me through glasses thick enough to be used as clear hockey pucks. "I know you're not used to going to a real school, what with your tutors and your mom homeschooling you on the road. But you're here now, and I want to help you do well at Davy Crockett. I want you to get a good education, make friends, and involve yourself in activities. However, your behavior isn't lending itself to any of those things, is it? Trust me, we all know you were a comedian, but now you're a student. Please, *please,* stop performing comedy at school."

"Maybe I have a slight problem with always being 'on' because of all my years on stage," I grudgingly admit. It's no fun hearing the truth about yourself. "I promise I'll try harder."

"Glad to hear it, Ginger." She smiles, probably hoping we won't have to go through this again, definitely ready to dig into her taco. "Now, do you have anything else you'd like to say to me before you head back to class?"

"Yes, I do." Sincere tears fill my eyes. "I do have something to say to you. I want you to know that I wish with all of my heart that I had made a better choice."

"Good." She quickly types a few notes about me on her computer. "I'm so happy you agree, Ginger!"

"Yes, ma'am, I do. Because I now realize that 'How do you make a cow quiet? Press the moo-te button!' is a way funnier joke."

Like I said, it's pretty depressing to bomb at 2 p.m. on a Tuesday.

CHAPTER THREE

I think about what Mrs. G said the whole bus ride home from school, the whole walk from the bus stop to our ranch-style house, and the whole way through our living room decorated by my parents with framed vintage rock concert posters (Dad) and southwestern pottery (Mom).

The horrible smell of baking tofu loaf assaults my nostrils as I approach the kitchen, so I'm not surprised to see my mom sitting at the table, on her laptop, as usual. I consider telling her about what happened at school, but she's focused on typing.

"Hi, Ginge!" she says without looking up. "Grab a snack, but make sure it's healthy!"

"So doughnuts filled with cigarettes are okay?"

But she's too busy to even turn around and give me an eye roll. I get closer so I can look over her shoulder and see what she's doing. Her screen is covered in pictures of sparkly rocks of all different shapes and colors. Green, lilac, pink.

"What's going on? Are you a geologist now? Or is it a meteorologist?" (I'm not doing very well in science.)

"No, silly. I'm having a big sale on healing crystals this month on the MindfulMommyNanci.com website. Be sure to tell your earth goddess friends about it because there are some great deals!"

"I would tell my earth goddess friends, or all my friends, if I had any," I mutter. I grab a bag of gluten-free pretzels off the counter and trudge to my room, wondering if there's a healing crystal named Quartz for Losers or something that I could rub on my feet to make me feel better about my mom ignoring my preteen angst so she can sell rocks online. If there isn't one, there should be. I make a mental note to send Nanci an email.

The thing is, my manager dropping me didn't just change my life. It changed the lives of my entire family. I wanted to find a way to keep working in comedy, but my parents decided the best thing for all of us was to stay put in Austin.

"We want you to have a normal childhood," my dad said. "You should be hanging out with kids your age. Playing soccer or something."

"Fine, I'll stay here and go to school," I'd reluctantly agreed. "Only because I'm too lazy to run away from home and you won't let me have my own credit card yet. But definitely no soccer because you know how much I hate organized sweating."

Anyway, this whole transition has worked out way better for them than for me. Now that we're not traveling all over the country for my gigs, they can do their own things for once (a computer job for my dad when he's not playing guitar in the Austin Dad Band and a whippity dippity New Age biz for my mom) and not just focus on me and my career.

Oh, right. My career. I should explain it a bit more. In a nutshell, it all started when I was three years old and repeating short comedy bits that I'd watched on television or Netflix or my parents' computers. It was fun. Basically just a party trick. "Ginger! Do that *Saturday Night Live* character for the neighbors!" my parents would say. Then I would do it and get applause and maybe a juice box or something. But then someone filmed me performing a few jokes at a backyard barbecue and tweeted it to Ellen DeGeneres, and Ellen showed the clip on her show. It was my big break! My (now former) manager saw me, loved me, and signed me on as a client. I was five years old. Five! I'd only been potty trained for a few years before I was standing on stages around the country. I lost my first tooth when I was doing a show at a club in Portland. ("Good evening, laydeeth and gentlemen!") I loved being a comedian.

Once I get to my room, I curl up on my comfy

bed with my snack and my sweet, fluffy orange cat, Applawse, who we adopted when I started school this year. She was a total bribe from my parents but a good bribe because Applawse is by far the best part of my new, humorless life. (And obviously I gave her that name because I love . . . applause and paws.)

"The thing is, Appy . . . " I sigh, petting her soft fur with one hand and feeding myself tasteless pretzels with the other. "The thing is that I've been trying to fit in at school, but I don't know how to deal with kids my age. It'd be like dropping you off at a kennel and telling you to go make friends with the dog squad and, oh yeah, join the kennel robotics club too."

Fun fact: I actually did try to join the Davy Crockett Robotics Club after Mrs. G told me it would be a good way to socialize. I went to one meeting and was confused the entire time because it was just a bunch of smart kids building machines and talking about math. "Do you have any questions, Ginger?" the teacher in charge had asked when she saw me staring blankly at a bunch of wires.

"Yes, I do. Why isn't anyone talking like a robot? I. Thought. That. Is. What. A. Robotics. Club. Does. Beep. Boop. Bop. We. Are. Now. Your. Machine. Overlords." Then I did some cool robot dancing with my elbows, and she nicely suggested I find a different club to join, maybe in another school district.

"I just don't think seventh grade is for me." I sigh again.

Appy stares at me with her big green eyes and doesn't say anything because she's a cat.

"I'm no good at it. I have no friends, and nobody thinks I'm funny, and I just don't know how to be around kids my age. But here's what's even sadder: maybe the comedy life isn't for me either. My manager wouldn't have dropped me if my act were still good. So if I'm not a student and I'm not a comic, then who am I?"

I can tell by her purring that she wishes she knew the answer.

CHAPTER FOUR

"Hey, um, is anyone sitting here?"

I look up from my Spanish homework to see Chance Reynolds, the totally cute boy who lives two blocks away from me in the house that always has broken sports equipment in the front yard, looming over my bus seat. He's never even glanced in my direction before, so I take a quick breath, look into his Blue Raspberry Icee-colored eyes, and answer as coolly as I know how.

"Si! El bus seat es muy bueno, my main hombre! Kamusta!"

Yep, the person who used to perform in front of hundreds of adults a night apparently now turns into Dora the Explorer when trying to speak to a boy classmate. Chance gives me a confused look and quickly walks to the back of the bus, where it seems to be a weirdo-free zone. I sit there, mortified by my inability to have a normal interaction with another kid. But a minute later, I'm surprised to feel a tap on my shoulder.

"Don't worry about him," the girl behind me with long, dark hair (who is wearing a . . . cape?) whispers. "Not everyone is multilingual. That means you can speak more than one language. Usually not at the same time in the same sentence, like you just did, though. Was that Spanish, English, and . . . Tagalog?"

"Maybe? Anyway, gracias," I say with relief. "That means 'thank you.'"

"I'm Daisy Rodriquez. I'm in your Español class," she continues. "So I got that one."

Three sentences! She just said three sentences to me! Short ones, but still, this is becoming the longest conversation I've had with a classmate since school started a few months ago.

"Nice to meet you, Daisy," I answer just like a normal person would. "Man, that was so cringe."

"Don't you mean *muy* cringe?" She giggles.

"Si, se puede, my hombre! Hey, if your last name is Rodriquez, why are you taking Spanish in the first place? For the easy A?"

"Maybe because my family has been in Texas for six generations and I've only been to Mexico once? How long has yours been here?"

Crap. I just blew it. As usual. But then, miracle of miracles, she actually stands and moves to the seat next to me. "What's your name? You're new, right?"

"Yes, I'm new. I'm Ginger Mancino. Middle name Nemo."

Daisy's mouth drops open, just like I totally knew it would.

I continue. "My mom lost the TV remote when she was pregnant and on bed rest, so she watched an all-day marathon of the movie *Finding Nemo*. Then, the next day, she was whacked-out on medication during labor because I was coming out feet first, so she told the doctor the first name that popped into her head—"

"So your name's Ginger Nemo Mancino? After an animated clown fish? That's brilliant!" Daisy doubles over in laughter.

Ahhh, my favorite sound in the world! I'm not surprised she finds that bit funny because I've been using that joke in my act for the past four or five years, and it always kills. But I'm thrilled that she, my possible new friend, finds it funny. Whew.

"So, uh, you're wearing a cape, I see." I try my hardest to sound casual.

"It's not a cape. It's a cloak."

"Oh, okay. Thanks for clarifying that. It's so hard to know the difference if you're not really into the opera scene. Did you, um, buy your *cloak* at Target? Do they have a new sporty wizard collection or something? Because it's like . . . super flattering and fashionable."

Daisy sees me wince on that last word and giggles.

"Relax, Ginger. I'm not a Harry Potter mega fan. I found this in the art room and thought it'd be fun to wear around today. It totally scares away the jocks, especially when I start mumbling nonsense curses at them. You should have seen Hunter Smith's face when I yelled, 'I summon you, toad army, beeple boople bop!' Hahahaha! Toad army. Like toads could carry weapons with their limited arm strength."

"Oh, thank goodness." I exhale. "That's great news! But one more question: Did you personalize your cloak with your name in gold letters? I mean, I'm thrilled that we're talking and all, but I need to make extra sure that you're not a kid magician with a personalized cape. Kid magicians are, like, the worst. I used to deal with them on the performance circuit all the time. Like my archnemesis, the Amazing Joshua. You know what'd be truly amazing, Joshua? If you didn't smell like a top hat filled with nacho cheese and old rabbit poop. Blechhhhh."

Oops. Did I just say all of that out loud? I slump

my head in my hands, filled with heaps of self-loathing, and wait for Daisy to get up and head back to the weirdo-free zone with Chance, where they can gossip about my possible alien DNA. And honestly, I wouldn't blame her if she does. Our friendship was good while it lasted. The best eight minutes of my year, in fact. I should probably scrapbook about it with my mom.

But for some reason, Daisy doesn't leave. She just sits next to me without saying anything.

The silence starts to make me uncomfortable for real, so I slowly lift my head and whisper bravely, "It's okay, Daisy. You don't have to sit next to me. I'm not going to cry or burst into a Taylor Swift ballad or anything. I understand that I'm not for everyone. I am what my parents call an acquired taste."

"Thanks for saying that, Ginger," she answers solemnly. "I totally appreciate it. And of course I *know* I don't have to sit by you, but I want to. You're definitely unlike anyone I've met at this school. I like you, and so does—"

I stare at her in shock as she suddenly stands up from the squishy bus seat and raises her arms to make the black folds of her cloak fly out dramatically like some kind of giant fruit bat. "The Amazing Daisy!"

We're laughing so hard, we don't even hear Mr. Luke, the bus driver, yell, "Hey, Dracula! Sit y'all's heinie down now!"

CHAPTER FIVE

I can't believe I'm saying this, but Daisy is like my *for real* friend now! Meaning she hangs out with me because she wants to, not just because she's being paid ten dollars an hour to be the kid comic wrangler who makes sure I don't eat too many Skittles in the greenroom then puke the rainbow all over the band leader's feet. (Seriously, how many times did I have to apologize to that guy? Like it was my fault he was wearing flipflops in December?)

And big news: she's sleeping over at my house tonight! My first sleepover! It's the most exciting thing I've done in the seventh grade by far. I told my parents earlier that it was okay to leave us home alone for two to twenty-four hours, but they had some issues with me being "only twelve" and "a minor" and "a kitchen fire starter." Whatever. Set off the smoke alarm a few times, and you immediately get a bad rep around this joint.

Right now, all four of us are out to dinner at P. Terry's Burger Stand in downtown Austin. Daisy and I are sitting outside under the oak trees at one of the little red tables, swatting at mosquitoes and waiting for our burgers, when she shocks me by saying, "Your parents are so much fun! I can't stop laughing!"

"*My* parents?" I pull a flabbergasted look. "You mean the people inside the restaurant harassing the fry cook about whether or not the vegetable oil is one hundred percent organic? *Those* parents? No, I don't think so. They're not fun."

"Yes, they are!" she insists. "My dad is totally boring and would never take me and a friend out on a Friday night because he goes to bed at 7 p.m. and he hates to hear the sound of children's laughter."

(Between us, Daisy's mom died in a car accident when she was two years old, so it's just her and her

25

dad. She doesn't really talk about it much, so I don't bring it up.)

"Look!" She shows me her phone. "I took a picture of your parents when they were holding hands. When we're old enough to have Instagram accounts next year, I'll post it with #OldPersonLuv!"

"Ewww." I move my hand to block the image from my eyes. "Can we talk about something more pleasant, please? Like that time I was backstage at a comedy club and bit into a peanut butter sandwich and found a toenail in it. A toenail! It was so gross. How does that happen, anyway? Did someone make the sandwich with their feet? Personally, I don't think I could hold a knife with my toes. What about you?" Okay, yes, an odd topic switch, even for me, but it's weird to hear my friend talk about how great my parents are when I don't always agree.

Daisy clearly understands my need to change the subject (friend mind meld!) because she holds up her phone again, but this time she asks, "Want to watch another one of your shows?"

"Of course I do!"

It's good to have a distraction while we wait for our food. The delicious smell of burgers and fries in the air is making my stomach rumble like a jet engine. I click around on her phone until I find one of the clips my mom uploaded to YouTube years ago. It was a performance I did at a retirement home when I was about eight years old. We push away the ketchup packets and put the phone in the middle of the table, then both of us lean over to watch me, dressed in purple corduroy overalls (WHAT?), standing in front of a hundred elderly people and riffing, "Being a kid is a lot harder these days than when y'all were young. You only had three channels on the TV to choose from and I have hundreds. Do you know how hard it is to pick a show? I'll be your age before I can find one!" Oy.

Daisy laughs a lot at the video, which is music to my ears. But after a couple of minutes, I hit pause because a wave of insecurity hits me. "Why did I used to dress that way? Why didn't someone tell me how awful my hair looked in pigtails? And why did I end every punch line with a fist pump like a pro wrestler? Those jokes are kind of childish, don't you think?"

"Yes, because you *were* a child," Daisy reminds me. "Stop being so neurotic, Ginger. Funny is funny."

I smile at her because I know she's right. I love that Daisy loves my comedy. And I'm a big fan of her passion too. Her passion isn't magician card tricks, thank goodness, but painting. Like, fine art painting, not houses. She's really talented too!

One day last week, between fifth and sixth periods, she asked me to come visit her in the school art room so I could see what she's doing IRL.

"What's that one called?" I pointed to a canvas completely covered with orange, red, and yellow explosions of paint.

"Isn't it beautiful? I know I shouldn't say that about my own work, but I'm really proud of it. It's called *Supernova Superego*. It's a commentary on how the tech world is turning our generation into rampaging nar-cissists, which will soon lead to our society's inevitable and fatal implosion."

"Oh. I thought it was about Fruit Loops."

"Yeah, that too."

I then walked to the other side of the classroom, where she had a ton of paintings leaning against the wall. She paints amazing portraits of people, like you'd see in a museum or something. Only I recognized these people.

"Wait a minute. Is that one of Mrs. G? And is that one of the lunch ladies?" I asked.

Daisy nodded. "I like to paint the people I see every day. I have about thirteen more, but I'm not ready to show anyone yet. Maybe someday."

They're all so good that I can't wait for everyone to see them!

Anyway, back to the burgers. They are delicious, and after we scarf them down, we get into my dad's truck and head back to our house. It's late, so we say good night to my parents, who I must admit haven't been too cringey tonight. They were actually kind of fun. Daisy even hugs my mom before we head upstairs to my room.

Once we're safely in my lair, I get into my bed, and Daisy settles into the pink sleeping bag on the floor. Applawse immediately jumps on top of her and purrs, which is super cute. He has good taste.

"So . . . now what?" I ask after a few minutes of silence. "What happens now at sleepovers? Are we supposed to do pranks and stay up all night? Braid each other's hair? Because I'm into it, but I'm also kind of tired."

Daisy laughs. "Honestly, Ginger, it's like you learned how to be a kid from watching TV or something."

"Yes, but that's only because I learned to be a kid from watching TV!"

Then, after I turn off my bedside lamp, I can't help myself, and my heart bursting out of my chest, I whisper to my new friend, "I'm so happy you're here."

"I'm happy I'm here, too, Ginger," she whispers back, then we attempt a high five, which isn't easy in the dark. But what is easy in the dark is being honest with my feelings, so I keep talking to Daisy, even though I can't really see her.

"Daisy, I know you're trying to sleep and that you like to get your full eight hours of snooze time, but can I tell you something before you nod off?"

"Of course," she says in a sleepy voice. "You can tell me anything."

"Okay, here it is," I start, then I unbottle what until now has only been in my head, and a stream of words pour out. "My dream is to be in the spotlight again. But since I can't do my comedy on a stage and it's impossible to do it at school, I don't know how to make that dream come true. Nobody laughs at my jokes, but it's the only way I know to get people to like me. I mean, besides you because you already like me. But you like everyone, and everyone likes you because you're so cool and you always help people if they need it. Which is awesome. All I have going for me is my comedy and my jokes. Oh, and also I think I have a crush on Chance, but I'm probably way too weird for him to like me back."

Daisy is silent, and after a few minutes, I wonder if she's even still here or if she rolled away in her sleeping bag after my word vomit. I hope she's not sliding down the stairs toward the front door.

"Ginger, thank you for sharing your dreams with me," she finally says. "You totally should have more friends because you deserve them! And more people should hear your comedy because it's so funny!"

"Thank you, Daisy. It's so nice that you—" I start to gush with relief, but then she sits up in her sleeping bag so suddenly that Applawse startles and jumps off to run into the closet.

"Okay, I got it!" she announces. "I've got the Ginger Plan for Davy Crockett Middle School Domination!"

"That was fast." I smile. "Let's hear it."

Then she tells me my new goals:

Goal #1: Prove to everyone that I'm funny.

Goal #2: Talk to Chance without acting like a freakazoid.

Goal #3: Text Daisy a lot.

Okay, so it's not a very intricate plan, and she's a little lacking in the details. But it's a start! Someone cares enough about me to make my life better. Both of us feel around in the dark for our cell phones, which our parents gave us with strict instructions to "only use responsibly or they will be taken away." That's fine with me because a lot of kids in seventh grade don't even have phones! We immediately achieve Goal #3 by texting each other about a hundred emojis each. Daisy loves texting, and I love it too. It's so much fun! Of course my mom and dad read all of my texts, but that's okay because it's not like I'm trying to hide anything. I'm not texting any government secrets to Russia! At least I don't think so.

As I drift off to sleep, I think about the other goals Daisy gave me. They're not as easy. Goal #1: Prove to everyone that I'm funny. How can I do that considering my personality limitations at school? Goal #2: Talk to Chance without acting like a freaka- zoid will be tough, but it's not impossible! I don't want to brag, but last week, I almost made Chance the Cutie (do not tell him I call him that) laugh on the bus three times. THREE. TIMES.

True, the first time it was because I tripped on a backpack and yelled, "What'd I ever do to you, back- pack? Do I owe you money?" and the second time it was because I asked Mr. Luke, the bus driver, if we could make a detour to Chill Zone because it was National Frozen Yogurt Day and I like to observe all major holidays. But the third time? I was standing in his way in the bus aisle and, in the voice that Prince William probably used when proposing to Princess Kate, he said, "Excuse me," and I panicked and said in a flight attendant voice, "Welcome onboard Davy

Crockett Middle School Air! Are you in first class, sir? Any peanut allergies?" and he almost made a noise that could have been a laugh. Progress!

Now I just need to figure out how to make five hundred other kids almost make a noise that could be a laugh. (Good ol' Goal #1.) Based on my middle school track record, it might not be possible.

CHAPTER SIX

It's Fish Sandwich Day in the cafeteria. The worst day of the week because nobody likes the school's fish sandwiches, so nobody eats much lunch, then they're all hangry (hungry + angry). Hangry means the jocks at the jock table get even noisier and rowdier, and the Crocodile Cafeteria Hunter can barely contain them.

When I walk into the lunchroom, I see that Daisy's sitting as far away as possible from Hangry Alley, thank goodness. She has a surprise for me as soon as I plop down at our table. I know this because her eyes are shining, her hands are behind her back, and she yelps, "I have a surprise for you!" Honestly, I should work for the FBI with these epic powers of deduction.

"What is it? Answers to the geometry quiz? Another cat? A brand-new car, even though I can't legally drive for four more years? Oh, I know! It's a hamster that poops glitter and rainbows! But honestly, even if it's just a serving of tater tots that you snagged before Jamal Thompson sneezed on the entire tray, I'd be happy because this fish sandwich I just picked up looks disgusting. Ew, is that an eyeball?"

"Nope, it's even better than germ-free tots!" she chirps, shoving a bright-blue flyer into my face.

Based on the tattered edges, it was yanked off the wall with a great deal of enthusiasm.

I pull the paper away from me so I can get a good look and read aloud, "Davy Crockett's Got Talent."

"Isn't that, like, perfect?" She claps and bounces up and down on the lunch table bench like a bunny who's had too much sugar.

"It'd be even more perfect if you put a question mark after those words: Davy Crockett's Got Talent?"

"Stop it, Ginger. It's totally perfect! The school

talent show is your chance to wow everyone with your comedy. Goal Number One! It's your chance to prove that nobody here can do what you can!"

"You mean accidentally wear their underwear on the outside of their PE clothes? Twice?" I pick up my fish sandwich then put it back down. I'm hungry, borderline hangry, but not enough to eat something that's looking back at me. Too bad the microphone is off-limits because that'd be a great Middle School Mystery Meat Show riff. Even the vegans would like it.

"Yeah, still not sure how you did that underwear thing." She laughs. "But at least now everyone knows that you have SpongeBob *lingerie*. Ha ha!"

My mind whirls. I know Daisy is trying to help me achieve Goal #1 like we planned during the sleepover, but the truth is that the past few months have made me wonder if I'm even funny anymore. My jokes are too young for me, and I don't have a lot of new ones. I want to be in the spotlight again more than anything, but what if I flop? I'm just about to blurt out all of that, but then I look at Daisy's smiling, hopeful, proud face, and my throat closes. I can't disappoint her. This girl has the biggest heart I've ever seen, and she believes in me one hundred percent. Which makes me wonder what's wrong with her.

"Daisy, can I ask you a question?" I'm suddenly shy. "And it's not if I can have the rest of your tots because I know you always finish them before the Cafeteria Crocodile Hunter gives us the five-minute warning. It's something else."

"Go ahead." She lines up her remaining tots in a symmetrical row. *Artists.* "What is it, Talent Show Star?"

"Um, I know you like me, and we had such a great bonding moment at the sleepover, but—*why* do you like me? I could understand if I were still kind of famous and you wanted to be my friend because of that, but I'm *not* famous. I'm a nobody. Especially in this school. But you? You're definitely somebody."

"No, I'm—"

"Remember yesterday at lunch when D'Andre offered to give you his half-eaten fruit cup? Or how Katie Lucas always waves to you in the hallway? Or how your photo is in last year's school yearbook as 'Best Artist' because tons of kids voted for you? Those things only happen if you're popular, Daisy. Everyone likes you. We've been having a lot of fun together, but I kind of don't get why you want to be my friend when you have so many other options."

Her smile immediately slides off her face, and she looks down at her lap for a minute. I feel awful for making her sad. Why did I do that? What is wrong with me! Did I just make her question being my friend? But then she answers in a quiet voice.

"Ginger, you make me laugh more than I ever have in my entire life. You don't know how much I need to laugh some days . . . like when my dad is lecturing me about my homework or about how much time I waste on painting or about a million other things I never seem to do right in his eyes. He just doesn't understand.

I know it's hard being a single parent, but it's hard being a single kid too. But now I'm not alone! Instead of going to my room and crying like I used to, I look at one of your funny texts or watch one of your videos, and I cheer up. You just make me . . . happy."

Like the sign I once saw hanging on a wall in a comedy club said, "Laughter is the Best Medicine."

We stare at each other for a beat with dumb grins on our faces, then she holds out her hand and offers me a tot. A grand gesture.

"You make me happy, too, Daisy," I answer while chewing. "It's nice to have someone in my corner again, cheering for me."

We're having a moment, she and I, right here in the cafeteria. One of the best moments of my life, in fact. Then a sixth grader named Emmilee trips and loudly splats on the ground, the contents of her lunch tray going everywhere, and the joint erupts in wild whoops and applause.

Huh. If these kids will cheer and laugh for that...

"I suppose I could do a quick five-minute set in the show. Then people would finally get me and invite me to things. Parties, pep rallies, pizza jamborees..."

"That last one's not a thing, but I like where this is going."

"And the school would finally stop sending emails to my parents about my 'adjustment issues' and my 'disturbing habit of calling all female teachers 'babe.'"

"For sure they would."

"Okay, I'll do it! But it's been a while since I've been on stage, and I get that my act needs some freshening up. So, if I write some new material, would you be willing to—"

"Watch you rehearse it? Your house after school." She smiles. "It's a date."

CHAPTER SEVEN

"Can I get you anything to drink, Daisy? Maybe some green tea? Your and Ginger's chakras seem a little out of balance this afternoon."

"Mom!" I'm embarrassed to discover my mom in full-on guru mode when Daisy and I walk into the kitchen after school. Trust me, the woman was a lot easier to deal with when she wasn't so enlightened. "We're *fine*." I give Daisy an apologetic look. "Daisy's chakras are top-notch right now. In fact, she just had them cleaned at the car wash last week."

"Ha ha." My mom turns back to her laptop. "Well, let me know if you need any essential oils to work on your harmony. There's a super great sale this week at . . ."

"MindfulMommyNanci.com!" Daisy and I chime in and laugh at the same time, causing my mom to shoo at us with her hand as we run off to my room. It's nice to have someone else around to experience the New Age madness happening in this house. I can't wait until she sees my mom doing a downward dog on the coffee table.

Once we're in my room, Daisy plops onto my pillow-filled bed, grabs a sleepy Applawse in a tight squeeze, then points her finger at me and commands, "Go!"

"Go . . . where?" I stand in front of her with my arms at my sides. "To the bathroom? I went at school after I chugged that bottle of water at lunch. Stall number three, if you're keeping track."

"No, silly! I mean, do your act! It should be easy for you. You make me laugh all the time."

"Well." I hesitate. "It's easy to make you laugh. You're my friend, and you have low standards. Kidding! But it's not as easy to come up with jokes for the show."

"Why not?" She looks concerned. "What's the problem? You used to be a professional. I've watched a gazillion of your videos online."

I hesitate. "I've been thinking a lot about this. The problem is that my old jokes about sippy cups and Play-Doh and Lunchables don't work now."

Daisy scowls at me for a moment, and I feel self-conscious, so I occupy myself by zipping and unzipping my purple fleece jacket. I don't want to disappoint her, but she must know that my Disney Princess lines ("Why is Cinderella so bad at tennis? She's always running away from the ball!") won't fly in a middle school talent show. These kids are way too sophisticated.

"Gotcha." She finally shrugs. "The old stuff won't work. So then hit me with something new! You must have some fresh jokes, right?"

"Um, sure . . ." I stall because I really don't. Just about the last thing I've wanted to do since the start of school, and therefore, my misery, was write jokes.

Any comedian will tell you that it's hard to create humor when all you want to do is hide in your closet and sing 80s songs with your cat. Yes, it's true that tragedy + time = comedy, but I've had way more tragedy than time. But I really want to prove to everyone that I'm funny, so I force myself to come up with something on the fly, aka improvisation.

"Okay, um, why was the middle school girl wearing all black?"

"I don't know, Ginger. Why was the middle school girl wearing black?" Daisy yells delightedly.

"Because her life sucks."

"Ginger!"

"Fine. Too dark. Hmmm, okay, what's the difference between middle school and a horrible flesh-eating disease?"

"Ging . . ."

"The difference is the horrible flesh-eating disease doesn't force you to learn geometry!"

Daisy laughs in surprise. "Hey, not bad! Not bad at

all! Applawse and I like that one."

"Really?" I smile, feeling my shoulders relax. I didn't realize how tense I'd been from trying to come up with something funny. Maybe Nanci was right about my chakras.

Feeling better, I try another one. "My parents took me to see a PG-13 movie the other night. And after they ate all of my popcorn, I realized that the PG stands for 'Parents Gobble.'"

Daisy shrugs. "Well, they're not all gems. But come up with a few more like the flesh-eating disease one, jokes that aren't too young or too old, and I think you've got yourself a new act!"

"Yay!" I cheer, then I take a running leap and crash onto the bed with her and Appy, who immediately startles and darts under my dresser. Poor thing doesn't know what to do when there's any enthusiasm or joy in this room. But still, I smile at Daisy, and my entire body feels lighter. It was like I was trapped under a heavy barbell, and now it's gone! Of course,

I'm not sure if she's right and this act will prove to everyone how funny I am, but as they say, the show must go on.

CHAPTER EIGHT

I'm standing behind the Davy Crockett Middle School performing arts theater's velvet curtain (which has been accumulating dust and teenage flop sweat since, like, 1905), peeking out at Daisy and Chance and my parents. They're all in the audience—not together, of course—watching the school talent show that I'm about to kill in.

The good news is that I was the only kid who didn't have to audition for the show based on my experience. Mrs. G made that happen for me. (Mad props, Mrs. G!) That gives me a little bit of star power tonight. The bad news is that the only people who've seen my new act are Daisy, me, and my dad when he was walking past my room to get to the bathroom. The other bad news is this: the last time I waited to go on stage was right before the worst moment of my life.

But as my mom would say, "It's bad karma to think about that," so I glance over at Miss Brenda, the mom in charge of producing Davy Crockett's Got Talent, to see what she's doing. Unfortunately, she doesn't think I have any star power, but that's only because her daughter, Blakely, is doing some hip-hop dance routine in the show, and she's hugely biased. (Nepotism runs rampant in the school talent show industry.) But trust me, I saw Blakely and her popularity pack at rehearsal yesterday, and I don't have anything to worry about. I've seen better dancing during Toddler Time at Gymboree.

The kid on stage finishes his act and gets some applause. Then a wave of unexpected nerves hits me, and my stomach feels queasy. I know I need to calm down, so I take some deep breaths like my mom taught me to do. Innnnn through the mouth, outttt through the nose. Or is it the other way around?

Ouuttt through the mouth, innnnn through the nose. Ugh! Why is mindfulness so hard on your mind? I shouldn't have to think so hard when I'm trying to breathe!

But my gasping seems to work, and soon my jitters pass. I know that after all of the rehearsing I've done with Daisy over the past few days, I'm ready. I hope that after my five minutes of great comedy tonight, I'll finally fit in. Or at least I'll move up in the ranks from "slightly more popular than the mop in the janitor's closet."

Once I get on stage, my job is simple: show everyone what Ginger Mancino can really do. I mean, if I can't kill it on a night when the best act is Jacob McCay doing a dramatic monologue from *Alvin and the Chipmunks: The Squeakquel*, I should just hang up my microphone for good.

"Now welcome to the stage, Ginger Mancino!" the emcee, Dev P., booms into the mic.

OMG, it's go time! I force a smile and run onto the

stage like a champ. Wow, it totally feels amazing to be back in front of an audience! The hot spotlight shining on my body is like a long-lost friend. This is the moment that will change my pathetic middle school life forever!

"Good evening, ladies and gentlemen," I begin after the polite applause ends. "Like the man said, my name is Ginger Mancino, middle name Nemo because my mom watched a *Finding Nemo* movie marathon when she was pregnant with me."

I pause for the laughs, but I don't hear any. I'm pretty sure my mic is working, so what gives? Daisy laughed at this joke when I told it to her on the bus! My cheeks start to feel hot, and a small bead of sweat forms on my forehead, which has never, ever happened to me while I'm performing.

"You know . . . the clown fish? His friend is Dory? 'Just keep swimming'? The reason I feel bad eating fish sticks?" I continue.

First sign you're bombing: you have to explain

your joke. The bead grows bigger and threatens to fall into my eyes. I slide into my usual follow-up joke to the Nemo bit, but my voice is a little weaker.

"The other reason she gave me that wild name was because the doctors loaded her up on heavy-duty meds that day. Why? Because I was coming out feet-first! Maybe I wanted the nurses to give me a pedicure so I'd be the cutest baby in the hospital nursery! Pink toenails, please!"

I pause once more for laughs, but again I'm met with a deafening silence.

Even worse, when I catch Mrs. G's eye, she mouths, "Just say no to drugs!"

Great. One minute into my act, and it's a complete and total disaster. The bead of sweat has now rolled down my face and is resting nicely on the very end of my nose like a shiny diamond of failure. Time to break out the new stuff.

I put my mouth to the mic that my sweaty palm is gripping. "Hey, do any of you know the difference between middle school and a flesh-eating disease?"

I wait a beat to give the punch line, but before I can deliver it, a kid yells from the audience, "My cousin almost died from a flesh-eating disease! He's still not fully recovered! There's a GoFundMe set up for him!"

"Yeah," someone else chimes in. "That's not funny!"

Heckling? HECKLING? It's a comedian's worst nightmare. The room is silent while I quietly panic. This is beyond horrible, and my confidence is shaken. But I quickly remind myself that I'm a professional. My years in comedy taught me how to read a room and get an audience back on my side. I know when it's time to switch it up and give the crowd what it likes. What it wants. And what this crowd wants is insult humor.

Ever since I started at this school, I've heard kids busting on each other. Then, to my surprise, after the insults, they all laugh and stay friends. I actually thought one kid's real name was Numbnuts because that's all anyone ever calls him. I make a split-second decision to improvise and do a little roast of the middle school. I'm sure they're going to love it.

I wipe the sweat off my nose and hold the mic to my mouth. "My favorite people in this school," I begin, "are the lunch ladies. Where else can you be served mushy peas and undercooked chicken by the Scowl Patrol? I mean, besides the county prison?"

I pause for a laugh, and I GET ONE. More than one, actually. A few titters. Okay, this is encouraging. But lunch ladies are low-hanging fruit, plus I actually like those babes quite a bit, so I decide to amp it up a notch. Go after some bigger targets. The popular kids. Dum dum DUMMMMMM.

"One group that I don't understand at this school, however, is the jocks. They're nice enough to let you cheat off of them but dumb enough that you'll get an F if you do! Hello, I'm flunking science now because I answered the question 'What is photosynthesis?' with 'A new selfie app' because I copied off of Trip Anderson! C'mon, Trip! Honestly, I think jocks are actually shaved bears who walk on two legs and wear jerseys with their names on them so they won't forget who they are. Roar!"

I eagerly look out at the audience, expecting to see people doubled over, laughing, but instead everyone just stares at me like I'm a slow-motion car accident. My parents, who are just a few rows behind a wide-eyed Daisy, look like they've seen a ghost, and my mom starts to kiss the crystal on her necklace like it's her new best friend. By the way her lips are moving, she also seems to be chanting one of her serenity mantras. Uh-oh.

"Blakely and her poodles will be out here dancing for you in a few minutes," I continue in a slightly weaker voice while pacing back and forth like a nervous tiger, "so that's exciting . . . if you're a fan of the uncoordinated. I've seen ninety-year-old grandmas with better dance moves! And they're using walkers!"

A gasp and an angry "What did she just say?" comes from the wings, where Blakely and her friends are watching. Yikes, I thought they'd think that was funny. Why aren't these insults as funny as the ones on the bus?

"Sorry, Numbnuts," I mutter into the mic and give Blakely a friendly wave.

That only seems to make her angrier for some reason.

The sweat on my forehead is now a total swamp, and my knees feel wobbly, but instead of stopping and saving what little social cred I have left, I panic and keep talking like there's still a chance at a comeback. "But I don't want to just call out the popular, accomplished, well-adjusted kids with bright futures tonight," I chirp. "No, I sure don't. So let's talk about the art students. Or as I like to call them, America's Future Fast-Food Workers!"

Oh, no. Oh no no no NO! What did I just *do*? How did that just come out of my mouth? I frantically scan the audience for Daisy, but she's no longer in her seat. The only people who come into focus for me are

my parents, who look both nauseated and disappointed, and Chance, who's definitely not smiling. Then my
eyes adjust, and I see about five hundred angry classmates who look ready to pounce. You know that phrase
"so quiet you can hear a pin drop"? That's how quiet it
is. Except for the pounding of my heart and the buzzing of the unused mic.

Finally, stage mom, Miss Brenda, pushes Dev P. on-
stage to grab the microphone from my hand. "Thank
you . . . Ginger, for whatever . . . social disaster that
was. Wow . . . good luck because you're going to need
it. Maybe think about homeschooling? In another
town?" he quips to huge laughs from the audience.

Really? *Now* they like insults? I dash off the stage
and immediately wrap my face in the stage curtain.
It's dusty and smelly and disgusting, but I don't care. I
don't want anyone to see how hard I'm crying. Now I
know for sure: my manager and the club owner were
right when they said I was washed-up.

Remember how I said that if I couldn't kill it on this

stage, I should hang up my microphone for good? I'm hanging it up.

CHAPTER NINE

Daisy's been trying to call me. Or at least that's what
my mom says. I wouldn't know if she has or not—probably not is my guess—because I've been holed up in my
bedroom under my big yellow comforter for the past
twenty-four hours. Pathetic, yes, but it's actually kind
of nice under here. I've even started to give the dust
mites names because they've become my new friends.
(Lil Sneezy is the sweetest.)

"Ginger, pick up your phone! It's ringing again!"

I poke my head out from my pillow fort like a
nervous turtle and see my yoga-panted mom standing
in my doorway. She and my dad have been very, very
concerned about my emotional health ever since the
talent show. They're even discussing sending me to my

mom's acupuncturist. At least that's what she told her twenty thousand Twitter followers.

"I'm not answering my phone again EVER," I squawk, hoping that'll send her on her way. I'm sure there's a quinoa cooking demonstration at Whole Foods or some other non-GMO activity to distract her for a few hours. Maybe there's a yurt that needs redecorating. But my protest apparently doesn't work because suddenly the covers are roughly pulled off me, and sunlight hits my body with the brightness of a thousand toddler beauty pageant smiles. "Ahhhhh! I'm melting! I'm melting! Turn off the sun, woman! TURN IT OFF. My skin is ON FIRE . . . FAH-YUR!"

"Oh, stop being so dramatic, Ginger. You're not a teenage vampire. You're too squeamish around blood, and we both know that dark colors completely wash you out. Now here, look at your phone. See that? Twenty missed calls from Daisy. Twen-tee. You owe it to her to either pick up or call back." She holds the phone two inches from my face, and I flinch like it's a live mouse with giant teeth, but she's right. I can see on the screen that Daisy has been calling every few hours today. Whoa. That's the most excitement my phone's ever had besides that time I butt-dialed the White House.

"Okay, I believe you, but tell me, Nanci Pantsi," I grumble while shielding my eyes from the super-intense sun glare. "Why would I do that? She's just going to yell at me for what I said about art students, and I already hate myself more than I ever thought possible. Do you know what it feels like to lose your only friend in the world? Because of your own stupidity?"

My mom gazes at me with an indecipherable look on her face, which is kind of weirding me out, but then my phone buzzes in her hand.

"Is it Daisy again?" I ask.

"Yes, it is. She just sent you a text . . . it says . . ."

"I don't care what it says! Text her back, and tell her I put on a sequined jumpsuit and fake eyelashes and joined a fancy circus! Tell her it was nice knowing her, but I'm Cirque du Soleil's problem now! I'm going back under the covers."

"You are being ridiculous, Ginger," she hisses. "And you obviously are having some low blood sugar issues and could use a nice açai bowl. But if that's what you want to tell her, why don't you tell her yourself? According to her text, she's here. At our house. Surprise!"

Two minutes later, I'm woozily standing in the middle of my bedroom, a vision of bedhead, dirty pajamas, and mismatched socks, when Daisy breezes in looking fabulous in a cute peasant top, jeans, and ponytail. How can she look so good when I feel so bad? She's also carrying a big black bag with her, which is a little concerning to me. But she only gets a foot inside the doorway of my lair before she stops near my hot mess of a closet and just stares at me. I'm so nervous to see her that I almost pee in my pj's, but here's the thing: she's not saying anything, but she doesn't look angry. In fact, it's not long before she breaks into an actual smile. And she keeps on smiling while I gape at her like I've never seen a real live human girl before.

"Day—zee . . ." I whisper after a few awkward minutes have passed. I'm so scared I'll say the wrong thing again, and that's exactly what I do. "Are you here to get revenge? Is there a pie in that bag? Like, a pie that's filled with poop that you're going to smash into my face? Because if you are—well, go ahead, sister. I totally deserve poop pie in my face because I am THE WORST."

I take a few deep, cleansing breaths, in through the mouth, out through the nose—wait, out through the mouth, in through the nose, why can I never remember?—then I bravely present my face to her with my eyes tightly closed. I feel like Cleopatra right before the Redcoats shot her during the Civil War. (I'm not doing very well in history class.) But guess what? Guess what happens then? I wait, and I wait, and I wait, and nothing happens.

"Come on. Let's have it!" I finally yell, opening my eyes and jumping up and down. "POOP PIE ME AL-READY! I'M WAITING! BRING ON DA NOISE! BRING ON DA POOP! SEND ME TO CRAP SANDWICH CITY, BABY! DOOOOO IT."

Silence. But then she finally giggles. What the what is that about? Giggling makes absolutely no sense unless she's laughing *at* me not *with* me. But at least she's not angry, which is a definite plus.

"Oh my goodness, I don't have a poop pie in this bag, Ginger! What kind of freak do you think I am? I don't even like *pumpkin* pie. Gag! Like I'm going to go scoop up doggie doodie then put on an apron and bake? You know that I'd never do that!"

"Okay, true. You do hate the culinary arts *and* dog parks. But if you really don't have a poop pie to throw at me, then what's in there? And why are you talking to me like you don't hate me for what I said in the show? You *must* hate me. *I* hate me."

"I don't hate you because I knew it was a joke,

number one. And I knew you were losing it up there on stage, number two. You didn't believe in yourself that night, Ginger. Instead, you said whatever you thought the audience wanted to hear. Insults? Seriously? It was a talent show, not the school bus. Listen, I've watched hours of your comedy videos, Ginger, and helped you practice, and I know you're never a mean person in your act. Or in real life either. Remember that rule of comedy you told me a while ago?"

"You mean 'punch up, not down'? Only make fun of people in power? Don't pick on things that people can't change? Oh, man. That's exactly what I did. Trip Anderson can't help that he's bad at school!"

"Yep. You panicked so much that you broke that rule. But it's okay. We all make mistakes."

"So you're not upset? Even about the . . . fast-food worker thing?"

"No, not even a little. I'm confident in my art. You know that. Besides, there's nothing wrong with being a fast-food worker. I ran out early that night because, well, I felt like it was my fault that you bombed. I was the one who told you to be in the show and who told you those jokes were super funny when you rehearsed them. Which they are! I don't know why nobody laughed. I thought *you* would be mad at *me*. Anyway, I'm sorry I wasn't there to give you a hug after you came off the stage. I'm sure you needed one."

"I DID!" I gasp, then I stagger-run toward her like I just finished a marathon and she's holding one of those silver blankets that make you look like a giant Hershey's Kiss. "Hugggggg meeeeeee!"

Daisy holds on tightly to me for a bit while I sob in relief, but then she finally has to free up an arm to grab a tissue off my dresser because I'm not exactly what you would call a non-mucus-producing crier. I can't believe how great it feels to have her here with me. It is the best feeling in the world! My friend is here! I keep squeezing until she gently pries me off of her, then she bends down to pick up her bag.

"Here." She reaches into it. "I made this to remind

you to always remember who you are."

I'm shocked when I see her pull out a big paint-ing! It instantly makes me start crying again, too, because when I get a look at it, I see that the painting is one of her portraits—and it's me. Or a more con-fident version of me, to be honest. I'm standing on a dark stage with pale streaks of yellow, orange, and pink light beaming all around my head like I'm a magical be-ing. I'm glowing. It is, hands-down, the best thing I've ever seen in my entire life. And I once saw a chihuahua wearing a tuxedo.

I. Am. Stunned.

"Daisy, I don't know what to say," I finally mumble, embarrassed that she did something so amazing for me. "Nobody's ever given me anything like this before. It's... just incredible."

"I'm so glad you like it!" She smiles, relieved. "I had to paint your face from memory because the only pictures I have of you are the selfies you took while wearing that creepy horse mask on the bus. Anyway, I know just where we should put this painting too. Right here next to your favorite thing, the picture of you on the Jimmy Kimmel show!"

She leans down and props the new painting up against my bedroom wall, right underneath the framed photo of me and Jimmy that's hanging there. She's right. It does look absolutely perfect. I finally manage to genuinely smile at Daisy, a smile from the bottom of my heart, and for a minute, I forget my sadness and my social failings and my nonexistent career. For a minute, I'm truly happy.

The Jimmy picture *has* always been my favorite thing in my room. Until now.

"So, will I see you at school tomorrow?" Daisy asks a while later, when it's time for her to go home.

"You sure will! I'm ready to be brave and face everyone!" I almost believe it.

CHAPTER TEN

It's the night before I'm going back to school, and I can't sleep. Daisy's visit earlier today cheered me up enough to think that I can handle whatever happens, but now I'm having big-time doubts. Will my classmates forgive me for what I said in the show? I honestly don't know. It didn't help that after dinner, I overheard my mom telling my dad that Mrs. G sent her an email that said, "FYI: the kids who hacked into the school website and posted a meme of Ginger's face with the words EPIC FAIL on her forehead have been disciplined." Oof.

After I toss and turn for what feels like hours, my dad pokes his head in to check if I'm asleep.

I sit up. "No, I'm awake, and also, I've thought long and hard about it and decided that I'm not going back to the seventh grade until I'm twenty-five years old. Thanks for asking."

"Look, sweetie." He walks up to my bed. "I know you had a bad experience that night on stage. But listen to me. You have to bounce back. This won't be the last time something like that will happen to you in your life." He adjusts his Keep Austin Weird T-shirt then sits down next to me and reaches his hand over to my head. I close my eyes and brace myself because I know I'm about to fall victim to the dreaded Dad Hair Ruffle that he's been giving me my entire life. He thinks it's cute, and so does Mom, and our assorted relatives, but whatever. None of them ever had to be dad-hair-ruffled then walk on stage at the Improv looking like the Lorax after he escaped from an industrial wind farm.

"Ginge, I know it's been hard on you going to a regular school, but I want you to know that your mom and I are so proud of you for trying." RUFFLE.

"Thanks, Dad, but I've been doing some research

and found out that lots of successful people stopped going to school when they were twelve."

"Like who?"

"Like . . . Michelle Obama?"

"First of all, not true. And second of all, it's just going to take some time." RUFFLE. "Comedy will maybe work out for you again, but you can't worry about that now." RUFFLE. "You'll find a way to fit in and make even more friends who love you the way you are, like Daisy does. And I'm not just saying that because we can no longer afford a tutor and your mom would lose her ever-loving mind if she tried to home-school you." RUFFLE.

"Yes, but remember my *G'Day with Ginger* show on the school PA system? The gig lasted two days, Dad. Two days. The principal got so many student and teacher complaints that I was yanked off midsentence on the third day. G'Day—ACK! Apparently, people thought I was 'too annoying.' *To middle schoolers*. That's like being kicked out of clown school for wearing too much makeup."

He and I look at each other for a beat, then he quickly nods, and I grab a piece of paper to write down the clown joke. We both know that one's a keeper.

"I'm just scared to go back, Dad. I have one friend, and that's awesome because it's one more friend than I've ever had before, but I just can't face everyone else at school. They *memed* me, man. MEMED ME."

My dad doesn't say anything then. He just reaches out his hand. RUFFLE. Then he whispers the worst possible thing he could say. "Wait here. I'm going to go get your mom."

Two minutes later, there's a knock on my door, and that knock can only mean one horrible, tragic, awful thing.

"Hello, sweetie!"

The earth goddess has arrived.

I slowly slide my comforter over my head. "Mom, I'm in the middle of something super important right now. Can you come back next week? I'll put it on my iCalendar, I promise! Bye!"

"Ginger," she says in her calm, Northern California voice as she glides into the room.

The calm, Northern California voice is the one she uses for yoga, meditation, and whenever she's talking to social-good-type companies when she wants them to pay her to write a review on her blog. When she's annoyed, like at the Austin Java barista for screwing up her nonfat chai latte for the third time, she uses her Texas voice.

"Ginger, I'm here because your dad and I just want our special girl back," she purrs. "We want you to have that confidence and HOOTZPAH! you had when you were younger. Remember that girl? Ginger Nemo Mancino, the famous kid comedian?"

"First of all, it's 'chutzpah,' not 'hootzpah,' Mom. Second of all, can you please just let me get back to fretting? I'm fine and okay and completely well adjusted, and I currently have no plans to get a sad face emoji tattooed on my back."

She doesn't answer, so I peek my head out and see that she's placing a big, rose-colored candle on my dresser. Huh? Do I seem like the type of person who likes rose-colored candles? The type of person who takes bubble baths and listens to the *Titanic* soundtrack for some "me time"? Um, no. I'm just about to tell her again to get out, when she takes a few purple crystals out of her pocket and arranges them around the candle. Crystals? Okay, this has to stop.

"If you pull a white sage smudge stick out of your other pocket, I'm calling 911, lady," I angrily tell her. "Now please take your hippie-dippie items, and leave me alone! Seriously!"

She ignores me, which is almost worse than when she gives me too much attention. Pick a lane, woman!

I continue to stare warily at my mom as she pulls a lighter out of her soft fabric pocket. She lights the candle and turns around to calmly gaze at me as I watch the flame grow bigger. "Ginger, stand up. And hold my hand."

"Ughhhhh." I don't move from my bed.

"GINGER, I SAID STAND Y'ALL'S BUTT UP, AND HOLD MY HAND NOW." And boom. Out comes the Texan.

I know enough to listen to *that*, so I yank back the covers and get up. Maybe if I just do what she says, she'll get whatever this "thing" is over with and leave.

"Fine," I mutter and reach for her hand.

She clutches it then closes her eyes and starts to sway back and forth while making a creepy humming noise. Of course, this isn't anything I haven't seen her do before—this chick performed a Swedish cleansing ritual in the middle of the Barton Creek mall food court last year after seeing a cockroach at Panda Express—but then she starts to chant some words that aren't even English. Or Spanish. Or French. Or whatever language it is they use on menus at Italian restaurants. No, she's chanting gobbledygook words and not in a multilingual way either. I turn my head and stare at her in horror. Is this what happens if you eat too much organic flaxseed?

"In a godda da vita . . . in a godda da vita . . . in a godda da vita . . ."

"MOM! SNAP OUT OF IT!"

"Thank you falletinme be mice elf agin . . . thank you falletinme be mice elf agin . . ."

"MOM!"

"In a godda da vita, baby . . ."

But she ignores me and just keeps on going and going and going. She's in full-on trance mode now. Like an extra from *The Walking Dead* minus the face decay and unhealthy eating habits. Yikes. If she doesn't stop, I actually *might* have to call 911. Or at least go get my dad to throw some ice water on her. And the candle, too, because the flame's getting higher.

Her eyes suddenly blast open, and the chanting stops. Thank goodness. I mean, I know she's a pain in my butt, but I still don't want to lose my mom to the cloud people or whomever she was talking to in that language. Aliens? Minions? Alien minions? But when I look at her, I can see that she's not entirely back to normal.

She still doesn't quite focus her eyes on my face, which is literally just an inch away from hers. Instead, she drops her grip on my sweaty hand, leans over to the candle, and blows it out, then she bows with prayer hands while whispering, "Namaste."

"MOM."

My shouting finally jolts her out of her daze, and she turns to me with a big, glowing smile and puts her face right up to mine. I wait for the explanation that I'm owed, but instead I get this:

"Oh, hi, sweetie! Uh-oh, looks like you're getting a pimple on your nose."

"WHAT THE HECK WAS THAT?"

"Oh, that? That was the Angel Ritual I learned at the retreat I went to in Marfa last month. Remember that one? The Womyn Womb Warryors Retreat? I brought you back a crocheted pregnant belly to keep your pencils in?"

"Yes, and I also remember that you came home and told me my spiritual guide is a three-legged weasel named Bodhi."

"Oh, Ginger, it was *magical* being out in West Texas in that spiritual vortex! Just magical. I learned so much about myself and how to harness my powers to help those I love. Like *you*. That's why we did this! Now, go to bed, darling, and when you wake up, the universe will forever change your life, and you will find better, more positive spiritual guides than Bodhi the three-legged weasel. I promise!"

Well, how the heck am I supposed to sleep after that?

CHAPTER ELEVEN

It took me a long time to relax last night after my mom's wacky babbling, but I must have finally conked out because it's morning, and I can feel both sunlight and dried drool on my face. The usual dynamic duo.

While I'm stretching myself awake, already dreading the school day but trying to face my fears about going, I hear my iPhone ping with a text alert. I'm guessing it's Daisy because she's the only person who ever texts me. Well, besides some guy named Louis, who texts me by accident because he thinks my number is Pizza Hut. I bend down to pick up my phone, and right away, I see two strange things: (1) the text is from Unknown, and (2) the text is a picture of Tina Fey.

Now, I love, love, love Tina Fey. She was the first

female head writer of *Saturday Night Live*, and she created and starred in *30 Rock* and wrote the movie *Mean Girls*, but why is she on my screen? Is she Unknown? Did she get my number from one of our comedy connections? That would be insanely awesome! Maybe she's writing a sitcom for me to star in! Or a movie! But then I look closer and see that the image is actually a meme graphic with a quote of hers typed underneath her face: *"Confidence is 10% hard work and 90% delusion."*

Huh. She really said that? Tina Fey? It must be something she said because there are quotation marks around it. (I'm doing pretty well in language arts.)

I'm not sure what to do. I mean, is this a prank? Or . . . could this be real? So I text back, "Is this really you, Tina?"

I stare at my phone and wait nervously for a response, but nothing happens. I wait another five minutes, and there's still no answer, so I give up and text Daisy.

Me: Hey! Did you just send me the Tina Fey thing?

Daisy: What Tina Fey thing?

Me: It's a picture of her and her quote saying confidence is 10% hard work and 90% delusion . . .

Daisy: It's not from me!!!

The weirdness of getting an anonymous text has my mind spinning, but I'm also thinking about the message itself. How could someone as hilarious and successful as Tina Fey actually say that her confidence is 90 percent delusion? I mean, have you ever seen Tina on TV or in the movies or hosting an award show? She practically bursts with confidence. She is *way* not awkward or shy in the least, and she is a total #LadyBoss.

I text Daisy back.

Me: Do you think I could pretend to be confident at school?

Daisy: TOTALLY!! FAKE IT TILL YOU MAKE IT, DUDE. COME BACK TO SCHOOL!!!! I'VE BEEN SO LONELY WITHOUT U!!!

Should I do that? Fake it till I make it? Like, trick myself into feeling like I'm a social success at school, and then I'll actually *become* a social success at school? Should I take Tina's advice and act delusional enough to get through a school day without crying or hiding in my own locker? I make a decision, and send one last thoughtful text to Daisy.

Me: 👍

Then I put my phone down and yell, "Moommm!"

After a few minutes, she pokes her head into my room. She has the glazed look she usually has after "quieting her spirit" in her "meditation nook" (aka the laundry room).

"Good morning, Ginger Nemo! I was just finding my bliss for the day."

"Okay, that's good." I stand up and shake the (literal) cobwebs off. "Mother, I plan to attend my public school today. Now, please bring the horses round and pour me a bowl of cereal. And chop-chop because I still have to get dressed and find my Lady

Speed Stick."

Her face breaks into a huge smile, which is nice to see, I guess, then she lunges at me for a hug. "Oh, Ginger, I'm so happy you're finally getting your old spunk back! I'm so proud of you! But, kid, there's no way you're eating cereal unless it's organic muesli from the farmers market."

I look into her eager, hopeful mom eyes brimming with emotion and swallow the first hundred retorts that pop into my head. See? I'm maturing already! I give her a weak grin and follow the advice my new pal, Tina Fey, just gave me. I squash all of my fears and doubts and worries, all of my "I'm not good enoughs" and my "I don't fit ins" and pretend to be confident about going back to face the middle school music. "Yep! I'm feeling great, Mom! Watch out, Davy Crockett Middle School, because Ginger's back!"

Okay, so I might have winced a little when I said it, but I still said it.

CHAPTER TWELVE

"Ginger! You're here! It's like Christmas and my birthday all rolled into one! Birthmas! Man, I wish you were wearing a giant red bow because that would be so rockin.'"

Daisy's is the only voice I hear when I finally step nervously onto the bus. Well, the only voice besides my mom's because I'm horrified to spot her chasing after the bus, yelling, "You go, girl! Goddess power!" as we pull away from the curb and turn onto the next leafy street. I don't know if Mom's excited because I'm finally facing my fears or excited because the house will once again be empty and she can crank up the heat and do her hot yoga in peace. Probably a little of both.

"Have a seat, kid!" Daisy commands, patting the worn green vinyl under her legs, snapping my attention back to her. "I've been saving your spot!"

I plop down, happy to not have to make eye contact with any of the other kids, who are probably glaring daggers at me. "Hi, friend," I say in a silly voice. "I'm Ginger. I'm doing a five- to seven-year sentence for refilling my soda when the sign specifically said 'No refills.' What are you in for? Grand larceny or credit card fraud or—wait. This is the bus to bad kid camp, right? Or did I get on the wrong one again? Gasp, am I going to—*middle school*? That's even WORSE."

This, of course, sends Daisy off into giggle-land, but I don't fully enjoy it because I'm still in a slight daze thinking about the text message I received this morning. My mind is reeling with questions: Who sent it? Why did they send it? Why did they send it to me?

"I'm happy you're back, Ginger," she says when she's done laughing. "It's been so boring without you."

"Thanks, Daisy. I'm happy to be back too. Yay!

High kick! Celebrate!" But even though my words are positive, something in my tone must sound off because she turns to look me up and down.

"What's up? You seem a little paler than usual. Like, I think I can see the veins in your forehead. Big, throbbing blue veins. Hey, can I take a picture of them to use for a future painting? Please?"

Because I'm a good friend and a noted patron of the arts, I nod then wait patiently while she snaps a close-up pic of my forehead veins with her phone.

"Daisy, first, don't actually paint that, but if you do, use glow-in-the-dark paint. Second, can we talk more about the strange thing that happened to me this morning? Like, it was really strange."

Unfortunately, I say that at the same time Mr. Luke, the bus driver, lays on the horn to show his displeasure at being cut off by a tiny mom in a giant SUV, so Daisy motions for me to repeat it. Mr. Luke is still angrily honking, so this time, I yell it as loud as I can so she'll hear me: "SOMETHING STRANGE

HAPPENED TO ME THIS MORNING!"

I don't think I need to tell you what happens next, but I will anyway because what else do I have to do? (1) Mr. Luke stops honking as soon as I raise my voice, and (b) Chance is in the seat right in front of us, only I don't realize it's him until he takes off his hat and turns around and looks at me with a small smile. Welcome back to school, Ginger!

I immediately slam my eyes shut and wish I were home under my yellow comforter with Lil Sneezy. Ugh. Today is as much of a crash and burn as I'd feared it would be, and I haven't even entered a classroom yet.

"I hate it when something strange happens in the morning," I hear someone say. Someone who sounds like—a boy? A boy who sounds an awful lot like . . .

"At least wait until the afternoon when I'm not so sleepy, right? But, um, what was it that was so strange?"

Chance? I open my eyes and see him still turned around in his seat, talking to *me*. Eek! Daisy subtly reaches over and squeezes my hand in excitement. Goal

#2! It's like I'm Cinderella of the school transportation system because the prince (Chance) finally noticed the lowly non-princess (me). I'm so shocked that he's talking to me, and this time it's not about blocking his way, that I completely freeze until I suddenly think of the perfect response to give him. But can I do it? Should I do it? Tina Fey's words flood into my brain again: Confidence is 10 percent hard work and 90 percent delusion.

Okay, Tina Fey, you genius. I'm going to pretend that I'm not the most nervous person on earth right now and see what happens.

"Well," I begin in my Austin drawl while looking right at him, "I would tell you what happened, but then I'd have to kill y'all, Chance. And the last thing I need today is a murder rap. Orange jumpsuits are so not my color."

There's a brief second of silence, then Daisy yelps with laughter. But Chance? He doesn't react even a little bit. He and I just stare at each other without any expression, and it's sooooooo totally uncomfortable. But I force myself to not look away or blush and be embarrassed. I force myself to act like I know that was a great joke. Because it *was* a great joke.

And then . . . seconds before I text my dad and beg him to send an Uber my way so I can get a one-way ride to Jupiter, the corner of Chance's mouth raises into a grin, and his eyes brighten with delight. "Yeah, you're right about that. You definitely look better in purple."

What happens after that I don't quite remember because a swarm of bees is buzzing in my brain, but Daisy tells me that when the bus pulls up to school, as we all get up to leave, I hug Mr. Luke and yell, "Confidence!" right before I trip on the stairs and fall out the door onto the sidewalk.

Awesome.

CHAPTER THIRTEEN

Despite my recent success on the bus, I'm nervous when I walk into my first-period class. It's filled with kids but kind of quiet. Creepily quiet, in fact. Why isn't anyone talking? Are they all waiting to ambush me together? I slink to the back of the room with my shoulders hunched, expecting to be hit in the head with a bunch of pencils at any moment, but nothing happens. Then I see Teddy Schumann sitting at my usual desk.

"You're back?" He looks up at me with squinty eyes. "I thought you decided to flee the country after the talent show disaster. That's for sure what I would have done."

"You're in my spot." I shuffle my Converse-clad feet

and try to at least sound confident. "Move. Please."

"You mean your ex-spot." He leans forward to stretch his skinny body over the desk and claim it with his boy germs. "This is *my* spot now, and I'm going to fart on it to prove it. Three, two, one—blast off!" PFFFFTTTTT.

Gross! I'm disgusted by the sound and the smell, but I'm even more disgusted that he gets laughs from the other boys in class! Scatological humor (that means jokes about poop, burping, and farting) is the *lowest* form of humor. Seriously, I work really hard to write good jokes, so it drives me bonkers when boys like Teddy just let loose a bodily function and get a laugh. There's no skill in passing gas.

But besides the fart attack, the rest of the morning is pretty uneventful. Except for the horror of my teachers giving me armloads of missed homework, that is. Working on all of the assignments will definitely hurt my social life, so it's a good thing I don't have one! I finally snap after my geometry teacher hands me a huge stack of worksheets to complete.

"How is learning about triangles even necessary in this day and age, Mr. Cross?" I bemoan, much to his delight.

He's one of my only fans in this school. He told my parents on conference night that he thinks I'm "a hoot."

"In case you haven't heard, sir, we have apps now. Apps that handle all of your shape needs. I think it's time I sent a strongly worded email to the Department of Education to let them know everything they're doing wrong."

"Go for it, girl," he drawls, leaning back in his chair and grinning. "Just be sure you print out a copy for us to hang up in the teacher's lounge. Lord knows we can't get enough of that outraged middle schooler humor! Ha ha!"

"I will! And I will use lots of exclamation points and semicolons in my email to make it professional too!" I huff my way out of the room, which only makes him chuckle harder. Man, I hate getting laughs when I'm not even trying. Although "outraged middle schooler humor" might be a niche to explore, now that I think about it. Maybe I *should* write all of my grievances down. As you've probably figured out by now, I have many.

It's finally lunchtime, and I'm waiting outside the noisy cafeteria for Daisy so we can walk in together. I am so grateful that I have her in my life because I don't think I could face this meal alone. No, I know I couldn't. An audience of five hundred adults drinking cocktails and waiting for me to make them laugh is nowhere near as intimidating as a lunchroom full of eye-rolling middle schoolers who may hate me. At least it's not fish sandwich day.

"Hey! Ready to eat something delicious?"

Daisy's happy voice jolts me out of my daze, and I look up from my shoes to see her smiling face atop a bright-pink sweater with a picture of a ninja kitten on it.

"Yes!" I reply. "I'm totally ready to eat something

delicious, but let's go to the cafeteria anyway."

She laughs and grabs my arm, and we head toward the lunchroom door. And then something both terrifying and, I'll soon realize, wonderful happens.

As we enter the crowded, smelly, and loud lunchroom, I notice Blakely and her clique of four girls (who I referred to as her "poodles" in the talent show) talking with a small, nerdy kid named Aanya. Except not really talking *with* her as much as *to* her because Aanya's sort of cowering against the wall while they surround her and point fingers in her face. I want nothing to do with this scenario, but it's unfortunately happening near the end of the food line, so Daisy and I have no choice but to stand right next to the drama.

Daisy notices when I immediately turn my back so they won't see me, and she shoots me a sympathetic look. She knows I'm not ready to face Blakely after what I said about her in the talent show.

"Admit it, Aanya! Just admit that you're obsessed

with us, okay?"

"Yeah, stop being such a loser and say it!"

"We've seen you following us around like a creep! You're obsessed with us! You're so pathetic."

I turn slightly around to see what's happening because, whatever this is, it sounds intense. Aanya looks like she's about to cry, and Blakely and the others have super-mean looks on their faces. Why isn't the Cafeteria Crocodile Hunter doing something to stop it? Isn't this what she's trained to do?

But then I hear Aanya's sad mutter, "I just want to be friends with y'all again. Like we were in grade school."

Ouch. Oof. That's for sure not going to make Blakely leave her alone.

Sadly, I'm right. It doesn't. In fact, instead of being nicer, Blakely snorts, "As if. Your mom *paid* me to be your friend in grade school, Aanya. Everyone knows that."

The poodles laugh viciously. This whole thing is beyond horrible, but I'm 100 percent going to stay out of the drama for my own protection.

Daisy? Not so much. She has another idea.

"Hey! Leave Aanya alone!" she commands in a super-loud voice. "You're all being awful!"

She's brave. I'll give her that. Brave and foolish, because at the sound of her voice, Blakely and the others spin around with red, angry faces to see just who had the nerve to stand up to them. This lunch has now turned into a bad preteen movie, and I'm the "dorky girl in need of a makeover" character just trying to not get stuffed into a garbage can.

"Oh, it's you, the *artist*," Blakely sneers, hair flips, sneers at Daisy. "This isn't about you, paint girl, so mind your own business, okay? Go sniff on some turpentine or something."

But then, just when I think that's that and we can move on to tater tot time, Blakely pauses, and I feel her icy stare on the back of my neck. Little hairs I didn't even know I possessed are suddenly standing up, and I feel bad vibes washing over me like a cold shower.

"Wait a sec—is that the *famous* comedian Ginger Nemo Mancino? The one who's so very, very famous that she ran off the talent show stage crying like a baby? Wah wah wah!"

"Leave Ginger alone too!" Daisy yells. Then in a quieter voice, "She just had an . . . off night."

Blakely and her friends smirk at each other and roll their eyes. "Ya think?" She laughs. "That was the worst performance I've ever seen. I don't know why you're wasting your time with her, Daisy. *You're* not a complete loser. But Ginger? Even Aanya would be embarrassed to sit at her table, right, Aanya?"

I can feel my face and ears turning hot, and probably bright red, while Aanya just shrugs in a sad way, smart enough to know not to answer that question. I stay quiet, too, figuring it's better to just take her abuse than to call any more negative attention to myself. Besides, she's kind of right. I'm the loser, not Daisy.

I walk away before anyone can see my eyes filled

with tears. But then behind me, I hear Blakely say this: "And by the way, Daisy? I've seen your paintings. You probably *will* grow up to be a fast-food worker."

Needle scratch.

Oh, no, she didn't.

My blood is boiling. I'm angrier than I've ever been in my life. Insult me? Fine. I'm getting used to it. But insult my friend, Daisy, who has done nothing wrong and who has the biggest heart on the planet? *I don't think so.* I whirl around and stomp back to the group with my hands curled into fists. I quickly un-clench them because I definitely don't want to punch Blakely. It's wrong to fight and not just because I have the upper-arm strength of a sickly kitten. But I have to stand up for my friend somehow.

I reach into my pocket and rub my thumb on my phone screen where Tina Fey was last seen.

Confidence is 90 percent delusion.

Confidence is 90 percent delusion.

Confidence is 90 percent delusion.

"Ahem." I look at each of them one by one. "Blakely, Blakely's poodles—I mean, Blakely's friends whose names I don't know but there's probably an Emily and an Ella in the mix—here it is: I'm sorry for what I said about you during the talent show. That was wrong. Your dancing was probably not the worst I've ever seen because I've been to a lot of my dad's middle-aged rock concerts. So I'm sorry for saying that. And I shouldn't have called you 'numbnuts' either. I apologize."

There's a disappointed murmur from the crowd of kids that's now gathered, because none of them were expecting me to be nice. The few kids who'd pulled out their iPhones to capture an amateur boxing video actually stomp away in disgust. But Blakely isn't impressed by my apology at all, and she scowls at me, her mouth ready to blast out a sassy response.

I jump in before she has a chance. "Also, there's nothing wrong with being a fast-food worker. So I apologize to all of them too. Especially the guy at P.

Terry's who always gives me extra fries. You're the real MVP, Manny! But here's the thing, Blakely and Emily and Ella and Emily: Y'all are mean girls. Like in the movie *Mean Girls* that Tina Fey wrote. You probably haven't watched it yet because it's PG-13 and your parents aren't as permissive as mine. But only mean girls would treat someone like Aanya and Daisy the way you did. And guess what mean girls turn into? Do you know?"

They all just stare at me with blank expressions, so I answer my own question.

"Mean girls turn into mean adults. For example! Know that lady who works at the taco truck on South Lamar? The one who calls everyone 'Señor Buttface' and throws hot tortillas at your head if you don't give her your order fast enough?"

Blakely reluctantly nods. Everybody in Austin knows Tiffany the Tostada of Terror.

"Tiffany was the most popular girl in the seventh grade when she went to school here. Her class president photo is in the trophy case by the gym. But then her meanness finally caught up with her, and everyone dropped her as a friend. Now she spends her days alone in a truck that never moves, and she will never realize her childhood dream of, um, being a hand model in France."

Daisy scooches closer to me and whispers, "Is that true?"

I want to whisper back "No" because it totally isn't, but I'm on too much of a roll to stop my electrifying speech.

"So if you don't change your ways, that's your future, mean girls. Trapped in a taco truck, elbow-deep in beans, with a face full of grease and hate. Meanwhile, 'losers' like me, Daisy, and Aanya, girls who didn't peak in middle school, will be living it up on our private island, drinking Diet Sprite cocktails, and horseback riding on the beach with our movie-star romantic partners who all love us and our multiple cats!"

I finish my performance with a flourish and a deep

bow and hear nothing but silence. Oh, man, tell me this isn't the talent show all over again, because I don't think I can handle that. But then I hear the smattering of my second-favorite sound in the world next to laughter: applause.

Okay, it's just Daisy and Aanya clapping, and a few other random kids and the lunch ladies, who may be doing it ironically, but it sounds awesome to my ears. And so does the "Whatever" Blakely huffs right before she turns on her heel and stomps away, her toadies following her. Huzzah!

Then, just when I think this has been one of the top ten moments of my life, it gets even better when I look over to the jock table and see Chance smiling at us.

Fake it till you make it.

CHAPTER FOURTEEN

Drama over, I'm ready for the rest of lunchtime to be easy. We invite Aanya to sit at our table, and she does! Unfortunately, all she wants to talk about is her online club that shares pictures of themselves dressed up like unicorns. (No judgment. Okay, a little judgment.) But she's still nice and sweet, and now she's my friend! That's a total of two friends, for those of you playing at home. Two! At this rate, I might have twelve friends by the time I graduate college.

"Did you see that Chance smiled at us?" I whisper to Daisy when Aanya gets up to put her tray away.

"Yes! That was really cool!"

"I guess that means he's on our side, right?"

"Totally. He's not like the jocks he hangs out with. Maybe it's time you had a real conversation with him," Daisy suggests.

I don't know what to say to that because the thought of a "conversation" with my crush is terrifying, but I'm still feeling pretty good. In fact, I'm feeling so good and confident about how I handled the Blakely showdown that I have an idea.

You see, I usually prepare my comedy in advance of performing it—like I did for the talent show with Daisy—but today I'm inspired to do something different. After all, all of that work I did on my act didn't do me any good. Like, ANY GOOD. Plus I liked how it felt to be spontaneous and wing it in the lunchroom. I liked just saying what I was really feeling, without any fear of being considered awkward or unfunny.

"Daisy, will you help me do something in the bathroom?" I ask her quietly. I don't know Aanya well enough yet to ask her to join us.

Daisy puts down her mozzarella stick and looks

slightly confused. "Sure. You need me to fix your hair?"

"Wait, what's wrong with my hair?" I ask, but she just laughs, and we stand up, say goodbye to Aanya, and head into the hallway.

Once inside the girls' bathroom (which always smells like lip gloss and hamburgers, for some reason), I guide us into the stall the farthest away from the entrance then position my body so that the gray door is behind me, not the toilet. I do have some manners, thank you very much. Then I ask Daisy to aim my iPhone camera at me and record while I just... talk. For two minutes straight, I talk about mean girls, taco trucks, peaking in middle school, and how some people think unicorns exist and you can order them online and ride them to school and that's okay. Basically, I sum up today's lunchroom drama as quickly as I can, and it's super fun. I don't think about what I'm saying. I just say it!

After wrapping up, I smile big into my phone's camera and chirp, "This is Ginger Nemo Mancino and my creative director, Daisy, reporting live from stall number four! Say hi, Daisy!" Daisy whips the phone around for a quick wave, then I flush the toilet with my foot because (a) germs and (b) it makes an awesome echoey Hollywood sound effect.

Flushing: the new applause.

We leave the bathroom, and I'm feeling happy as we walk back to the hallway before our next class. It was fun to just express myself like that. Freeing!

"Thanks for doing that video with me." I lean against a locker and finally exhale after the wild lunchroom experience. "It wasn't very polished or good, but it's something fun we can watch together later."

She hands my phone back to me and winks. "Remember when you gave me your mom's number in case, as you put it, you were ever lost in the forest and needed someone to rescue you via helicopter? Even though we both know you hate nature and that would never happen?"

"Um, yeah?"

"I just sent her your video!"

CHAPTER FIFTEEN

The next day, I'm busy trying to stay awake in second-period Spanish class when I get another text. Unfortunately, my teacher, Señor Tomkins, hears the alert at the same time I do, and he immediately heads my way. Sigh. It's my fault for not setting my phone on silent. And for choosing "Screeching Howler Monkey Party Palooza" as my text alert sound.

He arrives at my desk in less than .0002 seconds, pretty fast for a middle-aged language teacher, and stretches his arm out so his open palm is right in front of my face.

I don't even have a chance to get a good look at the screen. "Yes?" I ask innocently. "Es there uno problemo, patata?"

"You just called me a potato, Ginger," he says flatly. "Come on, you know you're not allowed to use your phone during class, so hand it over. I'm supposed to turn it into the office. Comprende?"

"Yeah, okay," I mutter. Out of the corner of my eye, I can tell that everyone in class is watching us with big smiles on their faces. Middle school kids love nothing more than seeing another kid get their phone taken away. It's like survival of the cellular fittest or something. I do my best to ignore their looks of glee and reluctantly surrender my phone to his hand. But right before I do, I glance at the screen. All I can make out is that the text is from "Unknown" again. Dun dun dun! Cue suspense music!

The last text from Unknown led to good stuff happening, so I can't wait to see this one. Maybe Unknown will reveal his/her/their identity! I strain my neck to get another look, but Señor Tomkins is already trotting back to his desk, where he puts my phone in a drawer and slams it shut. Whap!

THIS IS MUCHO AWFUL.

Not to be too dramatic, but *I might die without my phone!* I have to read that text! My hand is tingling with something like phantom limb syndrome, and I'm super close to hyperventilating. Eeek! I glance at the classroom clock above the door and realize that I have to wait thirty minutes until the end of the period to get it back. Whew. Thirty minutes. I can handle not having it for thirty minutes, I'm pretty sure, because—WAIT. Did he say he was turning it into THE OFFICE? To MRS. G?

Now in full-on the-brakes-just-went-out panic mode, I whip around in my desk and give Daisy, who sits a few rows behind me, a wild stare. My eyes are the size of dinner plates. Also, judging by the squish I hear when I move, I'm super sweaty too.

She shrugs and mouths, "The text wasn't from me." Then she gestures for me to calm down and breathe so I don't get in any more trouble. That Daisy. Always looking out.

I do what she says, even though it's tough, and squish back around to face the front of the classroom again. Innnnnn through the mouth, outttt through the nose. I relax and pretend to pay attention to Señor Tomkins telling us how to say "pumpkin" in Spanish. Then he ramps it up a notch.

"What do you think about that, Señorita Ginger?" he asks.

"Seriously? Haven't I suffered enough today? What I think is that today's lesson will come in handy the next time I spend Halloween in Mexico City and need a decorative gourd, Señor. I can't wait to carve a Jacques-o'-lantern this year!"

Before he can respond, the bell rings. As the class jumps up and starts to file out of the room, I quickly unwedge myself from my desk, grab my backpack, and run up to Señor Tompkins's desk as fast as I've ever run in my life.

"Señor—*Seen . . . yor*. Hold on a sec," I gasp. "I might need to take a knee here, 'cause . . . that was a lot of . . . physical . . . activity . . ."

"Your desk is cinco feet from my desk, Ginger," he says with a level stare.

"Si, Señor Tomkins. Yo conzeco . . . cozinco . . . consunko? I know that! But it es muchas importantes that I read mi messagios on my phone. Capiche, hombre?"

I lean against his desk for some rest, then my body starts to slowly bend toward his drawer where my phone is. It's like the phone and I are both magnets that can't live without each other. Which, I guess, we are (#iPhoneRomance). I'm just about to touch the drawer handle when he bats my hand away, so I stand up straight and decide to be honest.

"Please, sir? Can I have it back? My phone is really important to me. I have no social life, and my mom made me eat tofu doughnuts this morning, and um, maybe you remember the recent talent show?"

He shudders. "Yeah, that was rough. Really, really rough. But, Ginger, rules are rules."

"I know, I know, but if you give it back, I promise I won't ever use it in class again. I'll even turn it off before I come into the classroom. Please? It's like a beloved pet. Es uno gatito amour."

"What? It's a love kitten?"

"Dude, can I at least get some joy in my pathetic twelve-year-old life from my phone?"

He stares at me for a minute with an expression that I think is called "Does she need a medical professional?" Then he sighs and opens the drawer. "Obviously, if *you're* passing this class with that level of Spanish knowledge, I need to reevaluate a few things about my entire career," he mutters. "But I'm not heartless. I was a middle school dork who dressed like a farmer once too."

"What? These overalls are from H&M . . ."

He hands me my phone and waves me away. "Hasta luego, Señorita Ginger. Go get yourself some alegria. That means 'happiness.'"

"Eeek! Thank you! I mean 'gracias'! You're the

best! Au revoir, man!" I squeal, thrilled to have my phone back in my hand. Reunited and it feels so bueno! I mean, who knew that telling someone how pathetic my life is would work? Maybe that should be my new go-to move. "Yes, can I get an extra scoop of ice cream? I'm a seventh-grade disaster."

Smiling from ear to ear, I jog out into the hall-way, where Daisy is waiting for me, eager to see what happened.

"He gave it back to you? Whoohoo!" she cheers upon seeing me holding my phone. "He must think you're a great student."

"Yeah, something like that." I shrug. "But hold on one sec while I check my messages."

"Do you have tons of Hollywood offers because people love your new YouTube video? I saw that your mom uploaded it!"

I sigh. As if. "No, there are just three views so far, and I think they're all me."

"Then maybe you got another text from the famous

Unknown!" She smirks while I type in my phone's password. "Such a mystery!"

"I didn't just imagine that, Daisy," I huff. "That was a real text."

"Nobody has your number besides me and your parents. Hey, maybe Unknown is Louis, the guy who thinks you're Pizza Hut! Maybe he'll give you life advice about pepperoni today."

I ignore her teasing and stick my face into my phone. My nose is almost touching it when I see my new text. It's a graphic of Mindy Kaling's face—famous comedy writer, actress, author, basically one of the most awesome women ever—with this quote: *"Sometimes you just have to put on lip gloss and pretend to be psyched."*

Huh. What is that supposed to mean?

CHAPTER SIXTEEN

I'm so busy looking at my newest text that I don't even notice when Daisy heads off to her locker.

I feel a hand clamp down on my shoulder, and a raspy voice commands, "Get to class, my dear." I look up and see Mrs. G standing right behind me. The patterned tunic and velvet shoes she's wearing make her look like some kind of woodland nymph. A woodland nymph bent on destroying gentle, young souls. "You don't want to be late now, do you?" she asks.

I know it's one of those rhetorical questions that doesn't need an answer, but I answer anyway because I have opinions. "Well, actually, I kind of do want to be late because I have PE, and we're playing volleyball, and I'm terrible at volleyball, mostly because I don't have a killer instinct, at least that's what the coach tells me. I'm more of a lover than a fighter, you see, and . . ."

"Just get moving, Ginger," she interrupts with a tired smile. Then she lowers her voice a little and leans in. "And I'm proud of you for getting through your epic fail and coming back to school. That shows character."

"Thanks, Mrs. G," I mumble shyly then start to walk to class with my mind on my latest mystery text. What does that Mindy Kaling quote mean? "Sometimes you have to put on lip gloss and pretend to be psyched"? I think about it the whole time I trudge to PE, the whole time I'm in the locker room putting on my gym clothes, and the whole time I'm standing on the gym floor, playing volleyball with a bunch of athletic girls who could easily bench-press my dad. In fact, I don't stop thinking about the text until—

SMACK!

A volleyball to the face knocks me to the ground like a discount scarecrow. The big, echoey room falls silent as I lie flat on the smelly gymnasium floor, waiting for everyone to dash to my aid with a stretcher and a pint of ice cream. And maybe a get-well-soon teddy bear. Surely, they must be panicked that I'm injured and near death, right?

Nope.

"Gawd, Ginger, you suck!"

"Yeah, what's wrong with you? Pay attention to the game!"

"You just made us lose a point, dummy! Seriously, why does she always have to be on my team?"

Nothing like that middle school compassion to make a girl feel good!

"Ladies, move out of the way, and let me make sure Ginger isn't hurt," I hear from above. Is it an angel? Was I hit that hard? And why does the angel sound like a Texas woman with a three-pack-a-day smoking habit? The face of Ms. Delaney, our tough

PE teacher, who lives on a ranch and ropes cattle in her spare time, appears. She waves her calloused hand in front of my eyes, tugs on each of my ears, and pinches my nose. "Anything broken?" she drawls. "Am I gonna need to put you out of your misery, girl? Take you out behind the barn and deal with you cowhand-style?"

"WHAT? I'm not a BULL."

"Just tell me if you're okay, Ginger, so I know if I have to skip lunch and fill out paperwork." She sighs. "Are you going to live?"

"Barely," I moan from my position on the floor. "I think I broke my sphincter. I might need crutches too. And um, a doctor's note to never be in this class again. Also, a pint of ice cream. TIA, thanks in advance."

Suddenly, there's a loud thunk next to my head, and I'm startled into jumping up to stand. I'm on my feet panting, and my heart's racing. What was THAT? Did the ceiling collapse? But then I see Ms. Delaney slyly smiling and holding the volleyball she just launched next to my head and recaught. The lady's good. I'll give her that.

"Play ball!" she yells. "Ginger, now that you've made a miraculous recovery from the edge of death, you're serving."

Ugggggghhh. I hate serving because there's so much pressure to get the ball over the net, but what choice do I have now? I ignore the eye rolls and groans of the rest of my team, slowly plod over to her, and grab the white ball. Then I head to the serving line like I'm walking onto a gangplank. I'm just about to raise my hand and ask Ms. Delaney why the state insists on making us do physical activity when some kids really hate wearing shorts and socks at the same time (#middleschoolgrievance), but then it hits me. No, not the ball again. Mindy's advice.

"Sometimes you just have to put on lip gloss and pretend to be psyched."

Everyone in the gym is glaring at me, waiting for my weak serve so the game can resume, but instead of doing that, instead of failing and/or not trying once again, I shout, "One second!" and quickly reach into my athletic shorts pocket. See, I don't have any lip gloss, but thanks to my mom and her bizarre concern about my skin hydration, I just so happen to have a tube of free-trade, sourced-from-mountain-berries, all-natural healing lip *balm* with me. I hold the volleyball under one arm and rub that junk over my lips until they're fully coated and I smell like a state fair fruit pie.

"OMG, you are so weird," a girl named Ashley sneers. "This isn't a beauty pageant, Ginger. It's PE!"

"I know that!" I answer. "I know it's not a beauty pageant! That's why nobody's wearing a tiara and tap dancing to New Orleans jazz! But listen up, team: the reason I put on lip balm is because I want to look *goooood* when we kill these guys! Ready? Here comes the kiss of volleyball death! Mwah!" Then I throw the ball in the air, leap higher than I ever have before, and smack it down with my palm as hard as humanly possible. The ball soars over the net at rapid speed then boom! It crashes to the ground before anyone on the other team even gets close to touching it.

"Score!"

There's a one-second pause, then my entire team turns and stares at me with wide eyes.

"Yeehaw! Nobody saw that heat comin'!" Ms. Delaney hoots. "Y'all are a blue-ribbon heifer, girl!"

And then? Then the most awesome thing happens; my team starts jumping up and down and cheering. For me! Because I did something *athletic*. I have no choice but to jump up and down and start cheering too! For me! We're all cheering together! It's madness! Madness, I say!

Put on lip gloss? Check. Pretend to be psyched? Check. Have the best PE class I've ever had in my life? Check, check, and . . . check.

CHAPTER SEVENTEEN

PE class was over five minutes ago, and I've already changed back into my regular clothes, but I'm still floating on air from all the fun I had today. I think my newfound volleyball enthusiasm really turned things around for me. Two girls actually fist-bumped me in the gym. Fist-bumped! I thought that only happened to jocks and the people who won hot dog eating contests!

I'm so whipped up from what happened that I haven't even left the locker room yet. I'm just sitting on a bench, staring at Mindy's picture on my phone while I rest my never-before-used muscles. I gingerly touch Mindy's face with my finger, thinking how much her advice helped me find my inner confidence and not overthink, how it was the perfect thing to tell me. I feel great.

But I also feel confused. Who is sending me these texts? Daisy is right. Not that many people have my number. I believe her that she's not sending them, and I highly, highly doubt my mom or dad would. My mom is too wrapped up in her new career, and my dad only uses his phone to make phone calls, like we're a pioneer family in the 1980s. Is Unknown someone I used to work with in comedy? Or could it actually be Tina and now Mindy?

Only one way to know: I text back again. "THANK YOU, MINDY! THANK YOU THANK YOU!!!!! I SCORED A POINT WITH MY LIP BALM!!! Hey, is this really you?"

Then I hit the send button and wait. Tina didn't answer me, but maybe Mindy will. Nothing happens for a few minutes. My phone screen is black. I'm holding my breath. But then! Then those three gray texting dots appear like they do whenever the person on the other end is composing their answer text. Ugh! The three dots! The three dots of torture! I bounce up and down on the locker room bench, full of anticipation, and stare at my phone, waiting for the words to appear. What will she say? What will the answer be? And is it really her? It can't be, can it? She must be way too busy writing books and movies to text a middle school nobody. I lean back so I'm lying on the bench because I think I might pass out from all these questions racing through my head. I pull my phone even closer to my face and wait for maybe the best text of my life.

The three dots suddenly disappear.

Crap! Crap! Crap! Nothing! I thought I was finally going to get some answers about the mystery texts. I mean, I love the advice, and it's definitely helping me live my best life, but just who is doing this? And why?

I stand up to leave the locker room and go to my

next class, but then I realize something: I'm a little bummed about not getting a response, but instead of hiding and sulking and feeling bad like I usually do, I'm feeling pretty okay. In fact, I'm feeling inspired. So I shake out my hair, put my fingers to my phone, and text Daisy. "How fast can you get to the PE locker room?"

Two minutes later, she slams open the door and runs in. Pretty fast, I guess!

"Will you help me make another video?" I ask. "I just had a Summer Olympics moment in PE class, and I don't want to waste this inspiration."

"Of course!" she cheers. "I was just headed to the art room, but I can spare a few minutes for the *cinema*." We move around a bit so I'm in the best position to do my thing.

"And . . . action!" Daisy yells and pushes record on my iPhone.

"Hi, everyone! It's Ginger, coming to you live from the Davy Crockett Middle School girls' locker room!" I say into the camera. "It's just like the boys' locker room, except it doesn't smell like a skunk who farted out Axe body spray! Welcome to the middle school version of a day spa. Oh, and I'm not violating anyone's privacy because they're all gone. It's just me and the fungus in here right now."

Then I spend a few minutes talking about how I scored a point in volleyball and how that probably means I'll be playing in the Olympics one day, only I won't be playing beach volleyball because I hate when my sandwich gets sand on it, which is totes ironic, of course, SANDwich, then I stand in front of the sinks and say:

"Today I learned that if you try something you don't really want to do but act enthusiastic, it might turn out to be one of the best things you've ever done. DEEP THOUGHT, PEEPS. Now I better go because it's flu season and I have to wash my hands while I sing the 'Happy Birthday' song like my pediatrician told me to do so all of the germs die and I don't. Say hi, Daisy!"

Daisy turns the camera to herself, waves, then swings it back to me.

"Ginger out!"

CHAPTER EIGHTEEN

My mom is acting super weird when I get home from school. My backpack hasn't even hit the ground before she starts peppering me with questions like I'm walking on the red carpet and she's a low-level intern from E! Entertainment trying to get a sound bite about my new *Children of the Creamed Corn* horror movie.

"How was your day? Did you learn anything fun? What'd you have for lunch? How's Daisy doing? Is her painting going well? How much homework do you have? Was the bus ride comfortable?"

Finally, I've had enough of the inquisition. "Mom!" I huff, standing toe-to-toe with her. "What's the deal? Is your laptop broken? Why aren't you working?"

"Ginger, I always want to know about your day," she pouts. "I care about your life! And, um, yes, my laptop is on the fritz."

"Well, trust me, Mom. Nothing exciting happened today. It's school, not Walmart on Black Friday. I mean, sometimes there's a vicious brawl if the cheerleaders are giving away spirit cookies, but mostly it's just eight hours of being bored and sweaty."

She just stares at me with an odd expression, so I try to get past her using a spin move I saw some football player do at a University of Texas game once. Of course, it doesn't work, and I wind up twisting my ankle. Instead of giving me sympathy, though, my mom crosses her arms and shoots me a sly look. "Nothing happened, huh? Nothing? Or maybe *nothing but net!*" she teases, and I know I'm busted. How the heck does she know about the volleyball game?

"Fine, yes, it's true that I was the hero of the PE class volleyball game today, and now everybody hates me a little bit less. I'll probably get an endorsement deal with Nike or Gatorade, but it was no biggie. I definitely don't need you to take me to buy a sports bra so you can blog about it."

"Ginger!" She beams. "I'm so proud of you!"

"Thanks, but wait, how do you know about this? Ohhh, did Daisy send you my latest video?"

"She did!" She smiles. "I uploaded it to your YouTube channel, just like I did with the other one. I think it's so funny and great! So do a lot of other people."

"Really? How many followers do I have?" I ask excitedly.

"Let me think . . . including me, two!" She cheers.

Okay, that's a funny comeback, and now we're grinning at each other like a couple of dorks. She takes this as her signal to stretch out her arms and pull me into a tight mom hug, from which there is no easy escape. (But, um, the hug feels pretty good. Not gonna lie.)

"Ginger! My sweet Ginger! I just knew you'd start finding your way! I never in a million years thought you'd ever be doing sports with balls! But let us raise our arms and thank the Earth Mother for our bounty today!"

And with that, I'm dunzo. I know from experience that she's about two seconds away from bringing out her pan flute and tambourine and forcing me to join her in a solstice dance that makes us look like hippies in a hailstorm. It's happened before. So I carefully pry her strong yoga arms off my body and take a big step back.

"Well, thanks for the hug, Momarino, but I'm going to my room now to check out my newfound success," I tell her as coolly as I can. Then I head into the kitchen to grab a quick snack. Two people, including my mom, watched my video? That's the best audience I've had all year! I'm a rock star! (Note: this is called "self-deprecating" humor, where the comedian makes fun of herself.)

I lean against the kitchen counter for a minute, my mind spinning from the day I had, but then, out of the corner of my eye, I notice the rose candle from my mom's bizarre ritual sitting next to the toaster. I haven't thought of that night in a while, but boy, was that a weird experience. Then I have a wild thought: Wasn't the candle hullabaloo the night before I got my first mystery text? Is it possible that there's a connection between the whole candle/chanting/crystals rigmarole and the texts? Didn't my mom say I'd find new spiritual guides? Holy crap, are Tina and Mindy my spiritual guides? Nah. No way. I shake the wild thought from my mind. I don't believe in my mom's screwball stuff, and there's no way jumping around in my room with colored rocks could make comedy legends suddenly start to text me. Besides, I have better things to focus on.

Like my new video stardom!

CHAPTER NINETEEN

The next morning, I'm in the middle of an intense dream where I'm playing volleyball with Tiffany the Tostada of Terror (she's winning) when I hear a loud chirp.

"Go away, birdie," I moan. "I'm still sleeping."

Chirp. Chirp. Chirp.

"I SAID SHUT UP, BIRDBRAIN! I CAN'T TAKE IT ANYMORE!!"

Chirp.

My eyes fly open, and I'm prepared to yank the obnoxious tweeter out of his tree and wring his little feathered neck, when I see my phone on my nightstand. Then I remember that I changed my text alert to a chirp last night. *Because I thought it'd be more relaxing.* I stretch my arm out from under the covers and pick up the phone to see who's texting me.

Oh. It's just Unknown/Melissa McCarthy. No big deal.

Eeek!

It's totally a big deal because I love, love, love Melissa McCarthy! She was in *Bridesmaids* (which I haven't been allowed to watch in its entirety because it's R-rated and my parents have *some* rules) and the smash hit *Ghostbusters*. And whenever she guest hosts *Saturday Night Live*, her sketches are always the most hilarious ever because she's not afraid to let herself look completely bizarre to get a laugh. She goes in 100 percent and doesn't worry about what people think of her.

I sit up, rub my sleepy eyes, and focus on her text:

"Comedy to me is all about the bumps and bruises and weird tics."

Ha! That's a good one. Melissa is really physical when she performs, so I'm sure she's had tons of injuries. Me too. Like the time I was doing a set at a comedy club in Dallas called Laughs Y'all and some bad person threw his cowboy boot at the stage because he didn't like my joke about the Alamo. ("I was going to tell you a great joke about the Alamo, but I can never remember it.") The boot didn't hit me, luckily. It just knocked over my water bottle. So maybe that doesn't count because my only injury that night was thirst.

I'm just about to put my phone down and get up for school, but then I think about her quote some more. I've gotten faster at figuring out how these texted words of wisdom apply to me. Maybe she's not talking about actual bumps and bruises? Maybe she's being (language arts word alert!) *metaphorical*. Like the "bumps and bruises and weird tics" are actually the sadness and insecurities and self-doubt you have on the inside and express through your comedy. Whoa.

Methinks I need to rest my brain after that one.

I rub my temples because I seriously have a little headache from thinking such deep thoughts. Is this how those Robotics Club peeps feel every day? Ugh. I plop my head back on my pillow and close my eyes. I really need to get up and get ready, but after reading that text, I realize there's something more important to do. I grab my phone, hold it above my head, and hit the red record button.

"Hey, y'all, it's me, Ginger! As you can see, I've just come out of hair and makeup. I asked my glam squad to make me look like a middle-aged mom who's been up with a cranky newborn all night, and obviously they nailed it! Can you handle the hotness? Hold on—just need to rub a little sleep out of my eye . . . wow, that's as big as a pebble . . ."

Bumps and bruises and weird tics.

"Anyway, today I want to talk about perfection. I know y'all want to look perfect on social media. That's why right now, when I clearly don't look perfect, I'm making a video to show you that being real is better. I mean, think about it. Not a single one of us is always laughing and hanging out with friends. Sometimes we're home alone, and that's okay. I'm home alone *a lot*. No one is always on fancy vacations. Sometimes we're helping our dad wash poop off the cat's butt. No offense, Applawse! And none of us eats food that looks like the perfect Instagram shot 24/7. And if you say you do, I don't believe you. Look at what I'm about to eat—it's a pretzel that I found under my pillow! Yum! That's right, sometimes I eat the food I find in my bed. I call it the Mattress Diet. (Cough) Ugh, sometimes the food is fresher than other times. Need . . . water. But listen, people: be real. Let's all stop trying to impress each other, because nobody ever wins at that game. Let everyone see who you really are. And as you can clearly see, I'm a twelve-year-old who still sleeps in puppy pajamas. Ginger out."

I'm about to send the video to my mom so she can upload it, but then I hesitate because Daisy isn't here. She's my creative director and the woman behind the woman. We're partners! And to be honest, I'm not feeling as confident without her next to me cheering me on.

I hit "delete."

CHAPTER TWENTY

The past two weeks have been amazing! Like, the best weeks I've had ever since I started my year of purgatory at Davy Crockett. Daisy and I have made six more videos! They're all me riffing on a topic, like what it's like to start at a new school, things I love about my cat, what to do when your mom keeps nagging you about your "questionable hygiene," all relatable preteen stuff! Daisy helps me with ideas (and she and my mom do the technical part), and I couldn't do it without her. Since she's an artist, she's really good at knowing what looks good on camera too. (Purple top = good. Giant horse mask = not good, but only because it's hard to hear what I'm saying through the plastic.)

More exciting news: I'm up to one hundred followers on YouTube! I know some people have, like, a million followers, but I'm really excited about my one hundred. The video I posted yesterday about my shoes has almost fifty views! DogLuvvr98 even commented, "U R kewl"! I'm finally kind of meeting Goal #1, proving to everyone how funny I am. Just in a different way than we'd planned, I guess!

I'm so excited to get to school and talk with Daisy about more videos that I don't even argue with my dad when he tells me I can't have leftover BBQ ribs and coleslaw for breakfast. Then when I'm headed out the door to the bus, I actually hug my mom goodbye. With two arms. And a squeeze! I'm sure she rushed to her Facebook page to post a "Something's wrong with Ginger!" update. Wouldn't be the first time.

Alas, Daisy isn't on the bus when I get on, which is unusual. I send her a text asking where she is. I can't wait to tell her about my ideas and the fun we'll have making them happen. A few minutes later, she answers back and says that her dad is driving her this morning because he wants to talk. Huh. I wonder if everything is okay, but then she sends me a hilarious GIF of a squirrel chasing a ping-pong ball inside a bathtub that I watch on repeat the rest of the way to school. Seriously, what would we do without technology?

Midmorning, I make my way down the school hallway with a spring in my step. The smile on my face gets even bigger when a girl from my PE class nods in my general direction as we pass in the hall. It's not yet a "Hiya, Ginger!" but at least people are now acknowledging that I'm a human being and not a locker. Even Blakely is a little nicer to me when I interact with her in the girls' room before lunch.

"Oh. You. Are you in here to shave your mustache?" she asks when we find ourselves washing our hands next to each other at the sinks. "It's looking a little mountain mannish this morning."

"No, not shaving today," I answer. "Tuesdays are when I shave my mustache. Wednesdays are when I get my back waxed. Also, I hope you know that it's kind of patriarchal to say that women shouldn't have any unwanted body hair in the first place, Blakester. Give me my hair freedom!"

Instead of blasting a nasty comment back at me like she and the poodles are prone to do, she flips her long brown hair and leaves with a slam of the door. I consider that interaction with Blakely a win. It's like I finally reached an understanding with the neighborhood raccoon so he doesn't try to chew my leg off anymore and just rolls his eyes when he sees me. I'll take it.

I dry my hands with the dryer that has more power than an airplane engine then skip off to lunch to tell Daisy about the video I want to do this weekend. It'll have to be filmed "on location," meaning at Zilker Park, Austin's version of NYC's Central Park. Daisy's going to flip when she hears it!

Unfortunately, as soon as I get into the lunchroom and see her and Aanya at our table, I know something's up. Daisy looks miserable, and she never looks miserable. Not even when it's This-May-or-May-Not-Be-Chicken Day in the cafeteria.

"Hey, kiddo," I say with concern in my voice, and sit down next to her on the long cafeteria bench. "What's up? You look like I usually look. Wait, is it Opposite Day or something? Should I be in the art room creating a brilliant painting? Because if that's the case, may I request finger paints? Don't tell anyone, but I never really developed my pincer grasp. My secret shame is that I can't pick up Cheerios without a spoon. Sigh. I really hope that doesn't keep me out of the Ivy League."

She doesn't laugh or even answer me for what feels like hours, but then: "Sorry I'm so quiet, Ginger." Her eyes are downcast. "It's my dad again. He wants me to 'make some changes.'"

"To your . . . clothes? Is that what you mean? Or to your fingernail polish? Because what else would he want you to change? You're perfect. Like, it's annoying how perfect you are. Blech, am I right, Aanya?"

Aanya nods. "Word."

"C'mon, I'm not perfect, Ginger. You've seen the piles of dirty socks under my bed, and I had two cavities last year. But my dad's really upset that all I care about is art instead of my other classes."

"But aren't you getting all A's? You're a way better student than I am."

Daisy gives me a sad smile. "Yes, but he says it's time for me to stop this hobby because school is just going to get harder and I need to grow up."

Daisy puts her head down on her arms, and Aanya and I both gingerly pat her back. This is awful.

"Would it cheer you up if I told you the awesome idea I have for our next video?" I ask.

Daisy raises her head and looks at me with teary eyes, then takes a deep breath. "No, because I'm not allowed to hang out with you anymore either. He thinks you're a bad influence because your parents let you follow your dreams of comedy and now you're not doing well in school. He says that's what'll happen to me if he lets me follow my dreams of art."

Whoa. That's a lot to take in. Aanya and I stare helplessly at each other, not knowing what to say. Then I finally speak up.

"My parents didn't do anything wrong, Daisy! I mean, I know they're annoying and all, but my childhood was pretty awesome. Did you tell him that?"

"I did tell him." She sighs. "And he said a great childhood doesn't equal a great future and a good college. I also told him how much you mean to me, but he said he wants me to focus on my schoolwork right now and not art. Or you. Not even you, Aanya." Daisy gives a small smile to our resident unicorn.

"Oh," I say in a quiet voice and stare at my hands in my lap. "If you can't be my friend or Aanya's friend and you can't do your art, what are you going to do?"

"Just hang out with my dad and study, I guess," Daisy says. "I'm sorry I can't help you with your videos anymore. I wish I could because they're so much fun. Anyway, I have to go put all of my paintings in the storage room now. Ms. Chong, the art teacher, said she'll keep them there until the end of the year at least."

Daisy stands up and grabs her tray to leave. I feel a huge lump in my throat and tears pricking my eyes. My head is a bit woozy. I thought I felt bad after the talent show, and after my manager dumped me, but those times were nothing compared to this.

CHAPTER TWENTY-ONE

Despite Daisy's awful news, I show up to PE and still manage to somehow score three points in our volleyball game. Ms. Delaney stomps over in her big white sneakers and smacks me hard on my back at the end of class. "Good job, Ginger, you tough old steer! At this rate, you might not win the Least Athletic Student of the Year Award! Yipee kay yi yay!"

"They have that award? That doesn't seem very nice," I mutter. "But thanks for your support, ma'am." Then I scoot over to the water fountain because being an elite athlete makes you, like, super thirsty. I need to replenish my electrolytes or my electrobytes or whatever it is they're always talking about in sports drink commercials.

Finally, after my last class of the day, I'm standing at the bus loading area, thinking about Daisy and how it's so unfair that she can't do her art or be my friend. Me? A bad influence? That's ridiculous.

"Um, what's ridiculous?"

I glance over to my right and see Chance on the sidewalk, looking awesome in his khaki shorts and tie-dye T-shirt. Was he just talking to *me*? No, it couldn't have been me. He must have been talking to the flagpole or to his shoes or to a cloud or something. Surely not to *moi*. So I choose to ignore him.

"You said something was ridiculous," he continues, looking down at his feet and kicking a rock. "And I kind of want to know what it is, if that's okay. Ginger."

Holy crap, he *is* talking to me. I take a deep breath, turn to face him, and switch my brain setting from "hyper meerkat licking candy canes" to "normal girl acting normal." Yep, no big deal, just talking to the cutest person on the planet right now. (Inner scream!) I compose myself and reply, "Oh, was that out loud? Sorry, I was talking to myself. I do that a lot, talk to myself, but sometimes myself doesn't listen and ha ha ha! I'm so broke I can't pay attention! Now, where's that bus?"

For some reason, he doesn't move away. He inches closer to me like I don't repulse him in the least, which makes him different from, oh, pretty much everybody else at this school. I'm just about to ask him if he has me confused with someone else when he asks, "Were you talking to yourself about your YouTube videos?"

I'm so surprised by his question that I forget to "act normal" and just act normal. "Well, kind of." I step closer to him. "I have a great idea for my next one, and Daisy was going to work on it with me because she's my creative director and it's a two-person job. But she's not here because her dad picked her up, and she's, uh, not allowed to do things with me anymore. But you probably noticed that she's not here because you have eyes. Really, really blue eyes that remind me of a kiddie swimming pool. So, um, yeah. Ridiculous!"

I immediately shut my mouth and silently wish that Bodhi, my three-legged weasel spiritual guide, would suddenly burst out of the bushes with a giant net and drag me away from this embarrassment. I'm sure Chance is sorry he started this conversation in the first place.

"Can I help?" he asks quietly.

"Huh?"

"I said 'can I help?' Help you make your video?"

Whoa. *That* was completely unexpected. It would have been more expected if he'd started speaking French or break dancing or yodeling or something. Why would he want to help me?

"You're really funny," he adds. "I've wanted to tell you that for a while."

"Wha . . . ?" I shake my weasel dreams out of my head. "What'd you say? I'm really funny? Like funny ha ha or funny strange? Probably funny strange, right? That's kind of my rep around this place, in case you haven't been paying attention."

The corners of his mouth go up a little then, making him look even cuter. How is that even possible! It almost hurts my eyes to look at him, like he's the sun shining on a gigantic disco ball.

"You're funny ha ha, Ginger Mancino. Middle name: Nemo. And I think you're really nice too. Like when you stood up for your friends that day."

"I . . . am? You . . . do?"

"Yeah, you are, and I do. I wish I could be funny, but I'm not. And your videos are fun to watch because you're just talking, but you're funny when you just talk, and you give people good advice too. I really liked the one where you showed the organic flaxseed cake your mom made you eat. That was hilarious."

My first compliment from a crush, and it's about my mom's gross cake? I'll take it!

"I've watched all of your videos," he continues while I just stand and stare. "I know I hang out with the sports guys, but what nobody knows is that I'm actually a big film nerd. I think I might want to be a director one day. So I have a few ideas on how you could keep yourself in the frame better and use a different filter to make the lighting pop more, but—hey, here's the bus. Let's talk about it on the ride home, 'kay?"

" . . . 'kay."

Of course I'm still sad about Daisy, but you know that scene at the end of a romantic comedy when the music swells and the heroine has a huge smile on her face because her life will never be more perfect than it is in that exact moment?

That's the scene I'm starring in right now.

CHAPTER TWENTY-TWO

My favorite day of the week has always been Saturday. Back when I was performing, it was my favorite because being booked for a show on a Saturday night was a big deal. (Being booked for a 2 p.m. show on a Monday? Not so much.) And now it's my favorite because there's no school and I can do what I want all day long. That's why I usually wake up at 6 a.m. on the weekend, which annoys my mom to no end.

"Ginger, what are you doing up already?" she asks when she walks into the kitchen with bedhead and her yoga mat, probably on her way to do her first sun salutation of the day. "I have to drag you out of bed at 7:30 a.m. on school days."

"Yeah, I wonder why," I mutter, munching on my

granola. "Because you know how excited I am to get to geometry class and learn about . . . I honestly have no idea what I'm learning in geometry class. Hey, can you drop me off at Zilker Park around nine? I'm . . . meeting someone."

"Daisy?"

The mention of my best friend makes my face fall. "No, not Daisy. She's not allowed to hang out with me anymore because her dad wants her to focus on school."

My mom looks surprised. "Really?"

I squinch up my face and nod. "He also said that you and Dad indulged my career and it didn't work out for me because now I'm not doing well in school. So, he's not letting Daisy do her art anymore."

My mom looks upset and rushes over to hug me, which is nice. "Ginger, Daisy's dad can parent however he wants, but that doesn't sound fair to either of you. I'm so sorry, sweetie. But if you're not meeting Daisy at the park, who are you meeting?"

"Just . . . someone. Why do you always have to

invade my privacy? Just say 'yes,' okay?"

"Okay, okay." She gives me a questioning look. "No need to be rude, even if you are a hormonal pre-teen. That's not practicing mindfulness, Ginger."

"Sorry, Mom."

"And also, you're twelve. You don't have any priva-cy when you're meeting someone at the park, so I need the details."

She's right. And I know I wasn't super nice to her, but my emotions are all over the place. I'm upset about Daisy but also feeling nervous because the person I'm meeting at the park is—Chance! On the bus, we de-cided to film my video after his basketball practice. Of course, the meeting may just be some elaborate hoax where I wind up hanging upside down from a jungle gym while his friends throw rocks at me, but that's just a risk I have to take for the sake of my art. (And Goals #1 and #2.)

A while later, I'm sitting in our Volvo in the drive-way, waiting for my mom to come out of the house and drive me to the park, when I hear "Chirp!" It's a text! I immediately gasp with excitement because it might be from Daisy or Chance, but (almost even better) I look down and see it's from Unknown. I still have no idea who Unknown is, but I honestly haven't thought about it that much lately because I'm so busy with my videos.

I eagerly look at my screen and see that the text is a pic and quote from my ultimate favorite actor/comedian/director/funny person, Amy Poehler, star of *SNL*, *Parks and Recreation*, *Inside Out*, and a legendary improv performer. I LOVE AMY POEHLER SO MUCH. She is never, ever afraid to say what she thinks and is totally brave. I grin stupidly at the text picture of her little face for a second then read her quote:

"Girls, if a boy says something that isn't funny, you don't have to laugh."

Wait—really? I sure could have used that advice during my comedy career when I usually plastered a fake smile on my face so it looked like I enjoyed all of the dumb things my colleagues thought were hilarious. I never thought of *not* smiling. Not even when they were making fun of things I like, like women and cats. And in middle school, I've learned that if you don't laugh at the class clown (*always* a boy and, unfortunately, never me despite my obvious qualifications), everyone thinks you're a stuck-up butthead. It would be beyond awesome to say to boys like Teddy that his farts are not funny, but I don't think I'm as brave as Amy.

My deep thoughts on gender equality and humor are interrupted when my mom opens her car door and gets in, so I put my phone in my pocket and forget about it for the time being.

"Ready to go?" she asks. "Is your seat belt on?"

"Yep. Let's do it."

"Nice day today," she casually says as we fly down our street. My mom may be a gentle soul, but she's an insane driver. If she weren't so busy selling crystals and inner peace, she'd probably do well as a NASCAR racer. Or car thief.

"Yeah, it sure is. At least from what I can tell by the blur out the window. Hey, watch out! You almost hit that squirrel!"

"Sorry, Squirrel Friend! I wish you well on your journey!"

"You know that was a stop sign back there? Did you not see—how did you not see—oh my goodness, please don't kill me before I get my braces off, woman! I don't want to die with rubber bands in my mouth!"

"Calm down, Ginger." She takes a corner on two wheels. "It's bad karma to worry."

"It's also bad karma to crash into a tree, but what do I know? I'm not an internet guru like you."

We finally reach the huge green park and screech into the parking lot like the cops are after us. I see Chance and his friends on the basketball court. They whip around in alarm as we make our dramatic entrance, our tires spraying gravel in a twenty-foot radius. The Volvo finally comes to a shuddering stop, and I grab the door handle, ready to jump and roll to freedom. Before I can, the Mom Arm slams across my chest to stop me from moving, and I get the third degree.

"Is that who you're meeting? A classmate? Which one? They all look really sweet! Well, except for that one there with the cloudy aura. He's like a dark elf or something. Ask him if he needs a crystal bath because I could maybe give him a discount this month. But the other ones look nice! New friends! This is so exciting, Ginger! I'm going to park in the shade over there so I'll still be able to see you while I do some open-eyed meditation."

"Fine, thanks, Mom. And my friend is the one right there with the . . . bye!" I yell, hopping out of the car. Honestly, this is awkward enough without having to explain it all to her. I don't even really understand what's happening here myself.

Chance immediately waves me over, so I put on my brave face and nervously approach him and his friends.

I hope I don't have food on my neck or toilet paper stuck on my shoe, but I probably do. They're my usual accessories. I nervously glance at the squad as I walk over. I recognize most of them from school, from the jock table, but I don't know them very well. They're the ones who wrestle with each other during the "Pledge of Allegiance" then spend the rest of their day in detention.

"Hi, Ginger!" Chance cheerfully greets me. He's not as shy around me now that we've talked a few times, and neither am I. "We just got done playing ball. Guys, say hi to Ginger."

They all emit a noise in my general direction that's a cross between a greeting and a dying animal.

Then Chance says, "You guys remember Ginger, right? She's the comedian."

"No way! The one from the talent show?" Josh (Dark Elf) asks. "That's right! I remember you! You, like, bombed, dude."

"Thanks for the feedback. I love hearing from my fans."

"You want to know what you should have done for your act instead?" He smirks.

Great! Unsolicited advice! My favorite! "Um, no thanks, I'm good."

"You should have done THIS!" he yelps. Then he roughly sticks his right hand into his left armpit and pumps his arm up and down until a squeaky noise bursts out.

OMG. It's an armpit fart. An actual armpit fart! An armpit is farting! I seriously thought armpit farts were an urban legend, but apparently not, because it's happening right now in front of my face. I stare at him with a look of disgust. Not because it's a fart sound but because it's just really bad comedy. More of that scatological potty humor stuff. The rest of the guys clearly don't agree because they're all laughing hysterically. Except for Chance, who just smiles uncomfortably.

Josh finally stops his "act" then snottily says, "*That's* funny, Ginger." They all boldly stare at me, awaiting my response. I think about what Amy P. said: "Girls, if a boy says something that isn't funny, you don't have to laugh."

"Oh, my dear Josh," I respond sweetly and bravely without even a hint of joy on my face, much like my pal Mrs. G. "Did you know that armpit farts are probably the lowest form of humor that exists? They rank below burps, pee, boogers, spit, and of course, real farts. But nice try!"

The boys quiet down and look from me to Josh. They can smell the takedown in the air. I get the feeling that some of them would like to stand up to him, too, sometimes.

"Yeah, well, I don't think you're funny, and I think armpit farts are." His face is turning red, and I can tell he knows he lost some ground.

"That makes sense," I say, "that you'd think armpit farts are funny. Because based on a nature special I saw the other day on PBS, so do baby chimps." Then, as the rest of the boys double over laughing, I smile at Chance, lift my arm, and pretend to drop the mic.

Boom.

CHAPTER TWENTY-THREE

"Let's do it again, but this time, try to look like you're not going to puke."

"But I might puke."

"But don't."

"But I might."

"Ginger, just try your best, okay?"

"Okay. But you can't blame me if my breakfast goes downhill. It's called gravity. It's the one thing I actually learned in science class this year."

We've now been at the park for two hours working on my video. The first hour was taken up by Chance trying out different camera angles and natural lighting. After my mom walked over with some almonds and lemonade for a snack break, we sat at a picnic table, and he told me more about how he wants to be a film director someday. How cool is that? I told him about the directors I met on the TV shows I did, and he was super interested, asking me lots of questions. It's nice to have someone besides Daisy (and Applawse) enjoy hearing me talk about my former life!

Unfortunately, the second hour hasn't been nearly as fun as the first. See, the reason I needed help today is because I'm making this video on a teeter-totter. It was a great idea until I discovered that I have motion sickness. I know, what kind of person gets motion sickness on a teeter-totter? Answer: me!

From my position at the top of the teeter-totter, I look down at Chance, who sits at the bottom of the teeter-totter, holding my phone in front of him. It's still kind of surreal that he's here with me, but it's been really, really fun. He's super sweet and smart, and I haven't even thought about how cute he is for the last five, no make that four, minutes.

"Ready? Let's do this. In five, four, three, two—"

Chance silently points at me, and I put a big smile on my face.

"Hey, y'all! It's Ginger, and as you can see, today I'm up in the air! If I look a little green, it's because I'm trying really hard to not barf up my breakfast. Which was organic granola sourced in Guatemala, for those of you who are fans of my mother's cooking. Hopefully you won't see the granola come out of me in vivid Technicolor for yourself. Anyway, my stomach issues aren't what's important today! Today I want to talk about good days and bad days. Good days are when you're feeling high—not in the drug way, just say no!—but feeling high because everything is going your way. You get invited to a party. Your teacher forgets to assign homework. It's nacho day in the cafeteria, and you get to watch your favorite show after dinner. It feels great to be high! But then some days . . ."

Chance holds the phone as steady as he can while he slowly lifts his legs to raise his end of the teeter-totter and lower mine. He nods at me to keep going.

". . . you don't get invited to the party. Your teacher assigns, like, one hundred pages of reading. It's green bean casserole day in the cafeteria, and your parents force you to watch some educational programming about Belgian cheese-making after dinner. Or maybe, your best friend tells you she can't be your best friend anymore. And on those days, you feel . . . guess what? That's right—"

WHAP.

My butt suddenly smacks onto the ground when Chance lifts his legs too quickly. He gives me an apologetic look but motions with his other hand to keep talking. So I do because we're both professionals.

"Low. Low days can kick your booty. As we just saw. Oww, that hurts. I'm going to need a pint of ice cream. But trust me, people. I've had too many low days to count! Especially this week. Low low LOW."

Then I move my legs so I start to go up again, then down again. Chance and I continue to teeter-totter back and forth while I spout, "However, there's a famous stand-up comic and actress named Sarah Silverman—ask your parents if you don't know her, because she's amazing—who recently texted me, I mean, I saw a quote of hers somewhere. She said that in her life, 'I still have highs and lows, but maybe I don't cry salty tears as much.'"

(Sidenote: obviously I saw the quote of hers on my phone when Unknown texted it to me, but I can't really say that on camera, or people will think I'm even more of a nut than they already do!)

"Good saying, huh? It means that sometimes you're up, and sometimes you're down, but the important thing is to just keep moving instead of giving up and crying. Keep trying and doing your best because you'll never stay in the same place for very long and—OH NO, HERE COMES THE GRANOLA! Just kidding. I'm not going to puke from my motion sickness. Wait, maybe I am. Urp. OH NO. TURN OFF THE CAMERA, CHANCE. THIS WILL

NOT BE PRETTY."

I'm not sure if what happens next counts as a high or a low.

CHAPTER TWENTY-FOUR

It's now two days later, Monday, and that means school. Now that I have some friends, I admit that it's not as life sucking as it used to be. I'm finally adjusting a bit and haven't been called into Mrs. G's office in *weeks*. I wonder if she misses me.

I'm waiting on the corner for the bus, listening to the squawking birds and loud leaf blowers, and feeling super anxious to see Daisy and tell her all about Saturday at the park with Chance. I would have told her earlier, but for some reason (cough . . . her dad), she hasn't answered my texts since Friday. (Goal #3 failure) I finally stopped sending them after a while. Not talking to her makes me sad, but at least I have the success of my videos and friendship with Chance to distract me (Goal #1 AND Goal #2).

Here's the big, big news I want to tell her: the video we made on Saturday at the park is already up to (drumroll, please) six thousand views! Six thousand! It was Chance's idea to change the name from "Ginger Gives Life Advice" to "Texas Girl Pukes on Teeter-Totter." Brilliant! Who wouldn't watch that? It's so exciting, even though it's sort of embarrassing that tons of people have now watched me hurl up the contents of my stomach.

The bus chugs to my stop, and I hop on and eagerly look for Daisy. I'm hoping she didn't ride with her dad again, and I'm in luck because I see her in our regular seat. Yay! I hustle over, but right away, I can see she's gloomy again. Her little face is all cloudy and doesn't have its usual happy smile that reminds me of a puppy going on a walk. I hate not seeing her usual happy smile.

"Hey, Daisy," I say gently. "How are you?"

"Hi, Ginger," she says softly. "I'm okay."

I plop down next to her with my backpack and clear my throat. "So, um, how was your weekend? Did you do anything? I tried texting you, but—"

"Yeah, I saw." She turns to look out the fingerprint-covered window. "But my dad took away my phone so I could focus on my homework. Plus, from the texts I did see, you were doing more than okay."

"Wait, are you upset? About me making a video with Chance? I thought that was what you wanted for me. Goals One and Two! The video we made already has six thousand views!"

"That's great." She smiles weakly. "It sounds like you're finally getting famous again. Congratulations."

"Thanks," I answer, but it feels off. Like she's happy for me but not really happy for me? I'm not quite sure what's going on. Without her painting and her friends, Daisy has kind of lost her sparkle, while I'm finally getting back some sparkle. Why can't we both sparkle at the same time? I don't know what else to do but pat her on the arm, like a kindly grandma, and we sit in miserable silence for the rest of the ride. I'm so concerned about my friend that I don't even pull my phone out of my backpack to check my video views for the rest of the ride. But then I get an idea.

"I have to talk to you," I whisper to Chance as soon as we get off the bus and I chase him down.

Daisy has already trudged off to her first-period class, looking like the saddest girl in the entire world. She'd actually make the perfect goth if she weren't currently wearing purple polka-dotted leggings.

"Is it about Daisy? Because I heard you guys talking. I can't believe her dad still isn't letting her paint or hang out with you. So totally unfair," he says, and I try to suppress my smile because OMG isn't he just the best guy ever, ever, ever? Although he also seems to be a major eavesdropper, which could be a future problem.

"It's so unfair," I whisper until I realize there's no need to keep my voice quiet since Daisy's long gone.

"So, what do you think about us doing something to cheer her up and show her dad how much her passion means to her? I was thinking we could surprise her by making an art gallery of all of her paintings! We'll have to talk to the art teacher, and I'll see if my mom can let us use the garage for it, then we'll need to invite a couple of people, and we'll probably need some snacks but not chia seed ones because my body is probably seventy-five percent chia seed at this point, and maybe that's why I puked but—"

"I'm in."

"What?"

"I said I'm in. I think Daisy is awesome, and she's your friend, so I want to help. Just tell me what to do. But tell me later, okay? Because if I'm late to theater class again, the teacher will make me wash the finger puppets, and trust me, that's about the grossest thing on the planet."

He heads off down the hallway, and I smile while I watch him go. Operation Save Daisy is in the works!

CHAPTER TWENTY-FIVE

The past few days have been a blur of fun, hard work, and lots of laughing. We're actually doing a gallery show of all of Daisy's beautiful paintings! I want to hang them all up so we can walk around and admire them and say smart things about brush strokes and pigmentation, just like at a real art place in New York City. I can't wait to surprise her and show her dad how good she is!

"I'm happy you're doing this for Daisy, Ginger," my mom told me last night during dinner. "But just know that it might not change her dad's mind."

My dad chimed in, "That's true, Ginger. He's being protective, just like I was with you when I didn't let you quit school to tour with that sketchy improv troupe we later saw featured on *Dateline NBC.*"

"I know, but I have to at least try, right? That's what friends do," I replied, and then they looked proud of me, and I ran away before my mom could start up some sacred healing chants or something.

My parents are more than happy to let me use our garage for the gallery show, so Chance and Aanya come over to check out the space. Of course, this means introducing them to my mom and dad, but they're actually really cool. My dad only brings out family pictures once, and I'm able to knock them out of his hand before Chance gets a good look. Thank goodness because I was a really hairy baby. It's true! My family nickname was "Texas Hairball" until I turned two and started to molt a bit. Then he and Chance talk about my dad's band, and my dad even shows him how to play a few chords on his guitar.

More good news: Ms. Chong, Daisy's art teacher, is happy to help us get the show set up. "Her work de- serves an audience because she has a lot of heart and a lot of talent," she says when she opens the supply closet so we can see the paintings. There are a lot! It seems like Daisy painted portraits of almost everyone at school, even Dark Elf of Armpit Fart Forest. Then my dad drives up with his truck, and Chance and Aanya and I help load them all into the back. It's a lot of work, but worth it, I hope.

Chance has been awesome, of course. I keep saying how cute he is, and he is very, very, so very cute, but now that I've gotten to know him better, I realize how nice he is. I know "nice" isn't always an exciting thing to be, but what I mean is he's kind, considerate, has great manners, and he's willing to help a friend help a friend. He even had some great ideas for videos while we were shopping for party supplies at the downtown Austin farmer's market with my mom. (Luckily, he helps me talk her out of buying quail eggs because that's not exactly the snack vibe I'm going for.)

"Thanks for helping me with all of this," I say

to him shyly on the car ride back home, hoping my mom isn't listening. "I don't want to make this weird, but I'm honestly surprised you even talked to me, considering your friends are all of the popular jocks."

"That's true, they are." He looks down at his lap. "But that's just because we've known each other since kindergarten. They're not creative and funny like you are, though. I knew I wanted to meet you when I heard there was a kid comedian in our class. It just took me a while to get up the courage to do it."

The only thing *not* amazing this week is that I've had to avoid Daisy during lunch and bus rides (the only times she's allowed to see me) because I'm worried I'll spill the beans about the surprise. I texted her a crying baby GIF and told her that I'm behind in geometry and required to spend lunch in the classroom. My teacher wasn't too happy that I'm actually doing that, and he made me share my brownies with him all week to buy his silence. Is baked goods extortion

allowed in middle school? I don't think it should be.
#middleschoolgrievance

Last night, when Aanya, Chance, and I were hanging up the paintings in my garage, and I saw portraits of Mrs. G, the lunch ladies, and even a really cool one of Blakely, I realized that more people than us should get to see them all. Daisy always said that I deserve an audience, but so does she. A big audience! So I asked Chance to set up for a video, then I walked around the garage gallery and told everyone about what we're doing while he filmed me.

"Hi, y'all! It's me, Ginger. As you can see, I'm in a very famous art gallery that's attached to my house. The most recent exhibit here was my mom's car. Anyway, what you're looking at is a surprise we're making for my friend Daisy, who some of you may remember was my creative director before her dad made her abandon me for good grades and possible scholarships. Don't worry . . . there's no chance of her seeing this because she's not allowed to be on social media. Chance, can you zoom in on some of these paintings?"

Chance nods and points my phone at an awesome painting of Aanya in, of course, her unicorn hat.

"That's our friend Aanya. It looks just like her. Aanya is the one who Daisy rescued when she was being bullied in the lunchroom. Because the thing about Daisy is that she's kind to everyone, and she stands up for everyone."

Chance then follows me walking over to another painting.

"And this painting is of the person who bullied my unicorn friend. Blakely. But here's the thing: Blakely making a bad choice that day didn't stop Daisy from doing a portrait of her too. Isn't it pretty? Because that's Daisy's special talent: seeing the best in everyone. She definitely saw the best in me when most everyone else at school didn't. And that's why I'm doing this exhibit for her. Because Daisy literally saved my pathetic middle school life. And I hope that, one day, we can be friends again because she's amazing. Thanks for listening. Ginger, out!"

CHAPTER TWENTY-SIX

It's the day before the party, and I'm in the garage, making sure all of the paintings are hanging evenly. I made last night's video to show the world Daisy's awesome paintings, and I'm happy I did, but I'm still nervous about what she and her dad will think of this grand gesture. Or if they'll even show up at all because my mom had to concoct some dumb reason to invite them over. I sit down for a minute and think about my latest mystery text. The one from Issa Rae, star of *Awkward Black Girl* and *Insecure*.

"I wouldn't be anywhere without the Internet."

Which is true for her for sure because, before she was famous, Issa made her own YouTube videos, where she was just herself. Like me! They were a huge hit, and they led to her getting her own show on HBO and becoming a big deal. I guess that quote applies to me because of my videos, but what advice can I take from it? What lessons? Uh-oh, I'm doing some critical thinking here! Before I can figure it out, my mom and dad walk in with serious looks on their faces. Oof. Are they going to cancel the party? Did Daisy's dad find out about it and call them? Argh! I bet he did!

"Hey, what's up?" I ask nervously. My mom's serious expression is freaking me out. I can't tell if she's angry or sad or something in between. Same with my dad. This isn't looking good. I nervously twiddle my thumbs.

"We just had a phone call about you, and we need to talk about it," my dad finally says. I can tell he's dying to ruffle my hair, so I take a big step away from him. Safety first.

"Was it Daisy's dad? Because I'm having this gallery show no matter what he says!"

"No, no. That's not it. It's not about him."

"Whew! Then was it about the library book I haven't returned? Because I'm planning to do it just as soon as I find all of the pages that fell out after I dropped it in the bathtub and . . ."

"Y'all need to focus right now, okay, Ginger? FOCUS," my mom says in her Texas voice. Now I know this is serious. "The call we got was about the videos you've been making."

"My YouTube videos? But they're just of me being myself. You've seen them! You're the one that uploads them, woman! I'm not saying anything offensive or inappropriate, I swear. There's nothing R-rated or even PG-13. It's G-Rated City."

"We know that, Ginger. We've watched them all," says my dad. "And so, apparently, has the Jimmy Kimmel show. And they liked them so much, they tweeted a link to your YouTube page to their millions of followers, who liked them too. You've gone viral, Ginge!"

"What?" I gasp. "Wait, did you say 'viral' or 'virus'?"

"VIRAL."

I've been so busy with the party setup that I haven't really checked my YouTube account since last night. I even turned off the alerts. But could this be true? Are tons of people watching my videos? I was thrilled to have the few thousand who were mostly just there to see me blow chunks on a teeter-totter. I grab my phone and click on the app while my parents look over my shoulder. I scan to the last video I posted and look down at the number of views.

I'm confused. "Well, I don't know what you mean by viral. It only has a thousand views. That's fewer than I got on the last one."

"Ginger, look again," my dad insists with a gleeful look. "But this time, move your thumb because there are three more zeros under it. You don't have one thousand views. You have one *million* views."

One million views? ONE MILLION? I feel like

I'm going to pass out. This cannot be my life. How can this be my life? I feel dizzy all of a sudden, so I grab my dad's arm to keep from falling. But then I hear what my mom says next:

"Jimmy's producers want to fly you to Los Angeles to be on the show. Tomorrow night."

And I hit the ground.

CHAPTER TWENTY-SEVEN

When I open my eyes a few minutes later, I see my dad's blurry face inches away from mine.

He yells, "Put away the ice water and pint of ice cream, Nance. She's alive!"

Then I remember what happened right before I passed out. Jimmy Kimmel wants me on his show tomorrow! I'm back, baby! After the worst period of my life, Ginger the famous kid comedian is back. THANK GOODNESS.

My mind begins to race with thoughts about what I should wear on the show, what I'll say to Jimmy, whether or not I'll have time to eat at my favorite yogurt shop in LA, how jealous Blakely and the poodles will be, but mostly, how I can't wait to tell Daisy the news! She's going to die!

Oh, crap.

Daisy.

I look up from my position on the floor at her beautiful paintings hung up all over the garage and realize with a sinking feeling that the gallery show is also tomorrow. I can't be at both the Kimmel show and her party, can I? No! I don't have a clone! That's illegal! I sit up in a panic and instantly regret it when I wobble into a jar of shiny blue paint and knock it over.

"Mom, what am I going to do?" I'm near tears. "The party and LA are on the same day!"

"I know it's tough, sweetie, but it's up to you to decide. It's your soul's journey."

She reaches down and grabs my hand, the one not covered in blue paint, and pulls me up to standing so she can hug me. Then my dad joins in the hug, and well, it's kind of embarrassing, but it kind of feels amazing too. Like I'm in a Mancino cocoon that I never want to leave because then I'll have to make the hardest decision of my life.

Finally, they release me from their embrace, and my dad gently says, "You just have to figure out what's most important to you, kiddo."

"But can the gallery show be rescheduled? Can't we just do it another day? That's easy, right?"

"I don't think so, honey." My mom sighs. "Daisy's teacher, Ms. Chong, moved around her schedule to do it. Daisy and her dad are coming to our house under false pretenses, and I just announced another ChakraCon wellness retreat, so I'm going to need to work on my crystal displays in the garage for the next few weeks at least."

"Then do you think Kimmel will let me come on another day? Can we ask them? Please?"

My dad gives me a sympathetic look. "We did ask, Ginger, when they called. They're just fitting you in tomorrow, and they want you on the show while you're still viral. You've got heat, baby! Yeow!"

I don't know what to say or do, so I stand there

numbly looking at them with tears in my eyes. How am I supposed to choose between my best friend and my career? And the worst part is that I can't even discuss it with Daisy, or the surprise will be ruined. Ugh! What other twelve-year-old has problems like this? Maybe someone on the Disney Channel, but it's not like I can email the stars of that show *Dog with a Blog* and ask for help. I don't even know if that dog is online anymore.

I tell my parents that I'm going to go to my room so I can be alone and think, and I trudge away. But once I'm in there with the door shut, I grab my phone and text Chance.

"Did you see? Our videos went viral!"

"Dude, I know!"

"And the Jimmy Kimmel show asked me to be on . . ."

"GET OUT! THAT IS AMAZING!"

"Tomorrow in LA"

"Whut? but tomorrow is Daisy's party!!"

"I know. I don't know what to do! Being back on

TV would be the best thing that's EVER happened to me. But the party . . . what should I do?"

He doesn't answer me, either because he doesn't know what to say or because his phone is out of battery or maybe because he's lost phone privileges. But I don't text again because I know I need to just be by myself and do some thinking. Am I a bad friend if I choose the show? Am I a bad comedian if I choose Daisy? It feels like everything in my life is good, but everything is also awful. I'm back on the teeter-totter again.

I stew for a while, but at 5 p.m., I'm still no closer to an answer about what I'm going to do tomorrow. Show or friend? Friend or show? My mom said she needs to give the Kimmel people an answer by 5:30 p.m. This is really making my stomach hurt. I couldn't even finish the third tofu dog my mom brought me for lunch, so I'm probably down at least ten pounds.

Suddenly, my phone chimes with a text, and I

eagerly grab it, hoping it's Chance. It's not. It's Daisy.

"Hey babe hope UR OK!!! Miss you tons!!!! Don't tell my dad!!! Lol"

Should I answer her? Not answer? Send her the GIF of the koala who drinks Diet Coke then punches another koala? I feel guilty no matter what I do. But before I can do anything, another text pops up. It's from the famous Unknown again! This time it's a picture and a quote from one of my favorite stand-up comedians, Tig Notaro.

"Not many people have had as much bad luck as I have, but not many people have had as much good luck either."

Well, that's certainly true in Tig's case. After she was diagnosed with cancer, she didn't stay quiet and hide. She talked about it on a show one night and wowed the world with her bravery and humor. She is ah-mazing. But that quote maybe applies to my life too! I don't have the bad luck she did, but I still have some. Unknown always knows the perfect thing to say.

How does he/she/they do that?

I have had good luck with all of my experiences from comedy. I traveled. I was on TV. I met famous people. I made audiences laugh. I even got a free pizza after a show once (large with three toppings!). But I also had bad luck. My manager dropped me, and I was thrown into middle school, forced to spend my days with people who don't get me. And worst of all, I epically bombed in the talent show.

But then? Then I had good luck when I met Daisy on the bus and she became my first best friend. Then Aanya became my second friend. I definitely had good luck when Chance offered to help me with my videos and the party. And I'll probably have more good luck now that I'm feeling more confident and using my humor in my videos.

I grip my phone tightly, thinking. I know I won't get an answer, but I still decide to text back to Unknown: "Career or friend. Which should I choose?"

I put the phone down on my bed and close my

eyes to do some relaxing breathing. But then—

Chirp! A text alert. I glance down at my screen, and I can't believe what I see. Unknown answered me! The answer is another quote and not a real response, but that's at least something after months of no replies. I look at my phone and see Amy Poehler's face again with another one of her quotes:

"The earlier you learn that you should focus on what you have and not obsess about what you don't have, the happier you will be."

Wow. I read it a few times. It's similar to the good-luck, bad-luck quote, so I actually understand it without having to hurt my brain with a round of deep thinking. Unknown wants me to focus on what I "do have" and not what I "don't have" in my life. Let's see: I don't have my old comedy career. I don't have a manager. I don't have audiences paying to see me. I don't have a ton of friends.

But? I do have three awesome friends. I do have supportive parents. I do have a newfound talent for volleyball, of all things. Who the heck saw that one coming? I do have the courage to be creative and try again if I fail. And of course, I have my cat, Applawse. Can't forget that little furface.

Okay, Unknown: I get it.

If I do the show tomorrow, it doesn't mean I'll instantly become famous again. And even if it does, is that what's most important to me now? When it comes at the cost of losing Daisy and this new life I have? Shouldn't I embrace the bumps and bruises and weird tics of life that will make me a better person in the long run?

Out of the corner of my eye, I see something glinting and shining. I turn my head toward the light coming from my bedroom window and see the setting sun is streaking through the blinds right onto the painting Daisy made of me. It's lit up like a thousand-watt bulb, and it's beautiful. I didn't hang it up in the garage with the other portraits because it's too special to me. Now I stare at it and see my face the way Daisy sees it: full of vibrant colors, energy, love, and life. It's how I see her face too.

Then I look above the painting at the photo of me on the Jimmy Kimmel show.

"Mom!" I yell. "I made my decision!"

CHAPTER TWENTY-EIGHT

Is it weird to say that the best day of my life happened when I was twelve years old? I don't care if it is because it's 100 percent true that today is the best day of my life! No matter what happens in my future—if I win an Oscar, adopt a schnauzer named Bruce who water skis, then marry a chef named Bruce who also water skis—nothing will top today. And it just started ten minutes ago, when I woke up!

Because TODAY IS DAISY'S GALLERY SHOW!

In case you didn't pick up what I was laying down last night, yes, I chose my friend over fame and fortune. Of course I did! There was *no way* I could fly to LA to be on the Kimmel show if it meant not throwing

Daisy her party. We've been through so much together this year, and her friendship means the world to me. She supports me, no matter what I do (cough . . . talent show . . . cough), and I want to support her no matter what she does too. I hope we're best friends for the rest of middle school, high school, and college and then live together like Rachel and Monica on *Friends* until we're a hundred years old.

I know there's no way to do it in person, or if he/she/they even is a person, but I wish I could thank Unknown for helping me along the way this year with advice from my comedy heroes. They were all different messages, but they all taught me the same lesson: believe in yourself. I know, I know, that's like a cliché you'd see on a pink T-shirt at the mall written in glitter, but it also happens to be true. Believe in Yourself!

And yes, of course I know that Amy Poehler, Mindy Kaling, Melissa McCarthy, Tina Fey, Issa Rae, and Tig Notaro weren't *really* texting me. I don't know who was, and maybe I never will, but their words were for sure the inspiration and guidance I needed at this point in my life.

Maybe the texts were manifested because of some magic from my mom's goddess ritual candle, or they were from my imagination, or they're just a really strange feature of our AT&T data plan. I don't know. It doesn't matter. All I care about is that the texts made me realize what's most important to me: friends.

"Ginger!" I hear my mom yell while I'm brushing my hair. "Chance is here!"

Scratch that: friends, and friends WHO ARE CHANCE.

Two hours of hard work and sweat and finishing touches later, my parents, Chance, Aanya, and I stand in the garage surrounded by Daisy's paintings. All four walls are covered with them, and they are glorious! It almost feels like being at school because all of her paintings are people from there, but it's so much better because there's no homework and it doesn't smell like feet. All of us decide to sit down and have some snacks until Daisy and her dad show up, but then something strange and shocking happens: kids from school start to walk in through the open garage door. Whoa.

A freckled boy named Ethan comes up to us and says, "Hey, hope it's okay we're here. We saw your video, and we want to support Daisy."

"Yeah," says Jalisa, a girl from my PE class. "It's really cool you're doing this! Daisy is so nice."

WHOA AGAIN. WHAT IS HAPPENING?

"Thank you for coming!" I say back, then I turn and flash an excited grin at Chance and Aanya. "Grab some snacks, then go look at her awesome paintings!"

I'm shocked when I see more and more kids come in. It's like a bus dropped them off or something. The garage is filling up! Then I can't believe it. I see Mrs. G shudder up to the curb in Thor, her dented minivan.

She breezes inside, dressed in a tunic and capri pants, and approaches me with a satisfied smile. "This is so, so great, Ginger," she says with a hand on my arm. "I'm really proud of you, and I think I can safely say that after all these rocky months, you're finally . . ."

Then, together, we laugh and say "Adjusting."

"Thank you, Mrs. G. By the way, I think you'll like the painting over there in particular." I point to her portrait, which looks just like her, clear hockey-puck glasses and all.

She gasps, "It's me!" and runs over to take a few hundred pictures of it.

I stand quietly and look around the crowded garage, and I can't believe what I'm seeing. It's so amazing that all of these people are here at my house to support Daisy. My heart is full. Mostly. Because underneath my happiness, I'm still nervous about her and her dad coming. What if he gets even more upset? So much so that he moves them to another city? I walk over to the open garage door and try to remain calm before she gets here, then I feel a tap on my shoulder.

"Ginger, are there more pretzels?" asks Blakely.

"The boys ate them all."

"Yes, look under the table," I reply. *To Blakely*.

"Thanks," she says, walking away. She turns back to me with a small, almost-nice smile on her face. "I love the painting she did of me."

"Me too!" I answer. "You don't look scary at all in it!"

Then I hear a car pull up to the side of the house, so I turn and motion for everyone to shush. It's Daisy! Chance pushes the button to close the big garage door, and I walk out the small door and close it behind me. She has no idea why she's really here, so I have to be smooth. Relaxed. Chill. I give a small wave to her and her dad, who are sitting in their red sedan, and she gets out and walks over to me.

"Hey, Daisy! How's it hangin'?" I ask as casually as possible. I hear a low rumble of voices in the garage behind me and hope she doesn't notice. I kick a few pebbles to hide the noise.

"What's up, Ginger?" she asks nervously. "Your mom said there was something important going on with you and that's why we needed to come over here. Is it an emergency? Do you have mere hours left to live? That's the only way I got my dad to bring me here, so you'd better be bleeding from at least two places, or he'll be really upset."

"No, I'm not bleeding. But I could give myself a paper cut if you'd like."

She crosses her arms and gives me a searching look. "Ginger, is this about your barf video going viral? I know you've been really excited about becoming famous again. Wait, did your manager call to say she wants you back? Are you leaving?"

"What? No, I'm . . ."

"Am I here so you can say goodbye to me? Well, good luck. I hope you get everything you want," she says with tears in her eyes, then she turns around to walk back to the car.

Wait a second, this isn't the way this is supposed to go!

"Daisy! Daisy, come back!" I yell, chasing after her.

"Mr. Rodriquez, don't let her get in the car! I need her to go in the garage! She has to go in the garage! The garage is really important!"

"Hi, Ginger. Nice to finally meet you. You certainly don't look like you're near death," he says as he gets out of the car and slams the door shut with force. "I think I need to have a few words with your mom."

"I'm sorry, sir. I promise I won't bother you again. But this is the first and last time I'll ever ask you for anything. Let Daisy go into the garage. Please?" I implore, grabbing his arm. "For a minute?"

He looks down at me with the same big brown eyes that Daisy has and lets out an exasperated sigh. "Daisy, let's do what she wants, then we have to go," he commands, and they both reluctantly follow me into the garage. "You have that paper to finish."

"Thanks," I say, suddenly blasé. "Um, there's just a little something I want you to take a look at in here. It's like an . . . engine or a lawnmower . . . or a mouse or something . . ."

I slowly open the side garage door, and the three of us walk into the dark room.

"Ginger, what is this—" Daisy starts to say, but then I flick on the lights, and everyone jumps out and screams, "SURPRISE!"

The expression that pops onto her face is the best thing I've ever seen in my life! And I once saw a guy fall into a fountain at a fancy hotel and swallow a fish.

"Ginger!" she yelps, wheeling around to me. "Did you do this? Did you throw a surprise party for me?"

"Yes!" I yelp back. "I did! Because that's what best friends do for each other! And we're best friends forever!"

"But I thought you were going to go back to being famous." She smiles through relieved tears. "I thought you'd finally found your way back into comedy and you were going to leave me."

"Never." I grab her into a huge hug. "I'd never leave you." And I mean it. "But take a look around, Daisy. Because this isn't just a surprise party. It's a gallery show of all your work."

Then she looks at the walls covered with her paintings, and her jaw drops.

CHAPTER TWENTY-NINE

I thought the moment we all yelled, "Surprise!" right after Daisy walked into the garage and saw everyone from school and all of her paintings on display was the best moment of the party, but I was wrong. *Every* moment after that is the best moment. She's thrilled that we're all there to look at her art. The girl just can't stop smiling. I'm a little worried that her face might break.

"I think she's happy," Chance says while I'm refreshing the snack table. "And I also think we should have bought more food, but who knew all these people would show up?"

"You're right on both points." I grin. We glance over at Daisy, who is soaking up all of the fun and attention she's getting from the kids at school, plus Mrs. G and Ms. Chong. "Um, thanks for your help today."

He pats me on the shoulder awkwardly, then he makes the moment even more awkward by staring at me and clearing his throat ten times.

"Are you choking on something?" I ask, concerned. "Should I call 411? Where's my phone?"

"No, I'm not choking." He laughs. "Thank goodness. Because calling 411 wouldn't help me as much as calling 911 would. But, uh, I wanted to ask you something. Do you want to come over to my house for a BBQ tomorrow? With your parents?"

"Oh! Yes, I think that would be fun!"

He lets out a deep breath. "I do too! My dad loves music like your dad does, and I think it'd be fun for them to hang out. Do you think he'd bring his guitar?"

"He will definitely bring his guitar. We don't have a choice!"

We give each other dumb happy looks for a second,

then he waves goodbye and strolls over to take a picture of Mrs. G, who is still standing next to her portrait. We might have to drag her out of here later.

I whirl around to find Daisy but instead walk face-first into Daisy's dad's big chest. Uh-oh. I kind of forgot about him with the excitement of the party. He's probably not very happy that I did this, and I hope he's not going to yell at me. I cringe and take a step back, waiting for the lecture. Waiting for him to tell me he was right about me being a bad influence. He fixes me with a silent stare.

"Sir, I'm sorry that I did this without telling you first. But that's the only thing I'm sorry about because Daisy works really, really hard at everything. Not just her art. She also has straight A's, and she's always nice to everyone, and that counts for a lot. Look around, and you'll see what I'm talking about. Her paintings are beautiful, but look at how they make people feel."

He doesn't say anything, so I continue. "None of the people here were asked to come. They just watched the video where I talked about what a great friend Daisy has been to me, and to them, and they showed up to support her. And I think you should too."

Suddenly, I feel him grab me, and he pulls me into a big bear hug. I smell his comforting dad smell. It's like a forest mixed with coffee. "Thank you, Ginger," he whispers into my ear. "Thank you for doing this for my daughter. I had no idea that she had so many friends. The look on her face when she walked in was unbelievable."

"You're welcome," I mutter, my face pressed against his white guayabera shirt and my lungs straining to breathe. "No problemo."

"I know I can be too hard on her," he says softly as he releases his grip. "Ever since her mom passed away, the only person she's had in the world is me. I just love her so much that I want to make sure her life is successful."

"But it is. Look around!"

He lets go of me then and smiles sweetly. "She's

pretty talented, huh?"

"Big-time."

"Thanks for reminding me of that, kiddo," he says. "I'm not too proud to admit when I'm wrong." Then he whams my back with his huge hand and walks over to hug a beaming Daisy, who just watched the whole scene unfold. Neither one of us can stop smiling.

"Thanks, BFF," Daisy says to me after she leaves her dad chatting with Ms. Chong. "This is the nicest thing anyone has ever done for me."

"If you think that's nice, just wait!" I reply, then I run over and grab a package for her to unwrap. "I almost forgot to give you this."

Daisy squeals then excitedly tears off the bright-pink-and-purple wrapping paper. Her face immediately lights up when she sees what's inside. "I can't believe you did this!" she yelps and pulls a pile of shiny black material out of the box. "My own personal cloak!"

"Before you put it on, look at the back," I tell her.

She turns the drapey fabric around and there, in big glittery letters, are the words THE AMAZING DAISY.

"Just promise me you won't do any magic, okay? Not even a little. I mean it."

After I eat a bunch of snacks and talk to a bunch of people, I step off to the side of the party to take in everything. I see friends that I didn't have even last week having a great time in my garage. I see my parents, who are always #TeamGinger, who helped me pull this off. I see Mrs. G give me a proud smile, no doubt taking credit for me not being a delinquent. And I see Daisy in her big black cloak and her dad smiling at her paintings and holding her hand. My heart feels like it's growing three sizes, just like the Grinch's. Then I see Chance and Aanya, who helped me put all of this together, and both of them wave to me.

Who needs Jimmy Kimmel, anyway?

I grab my phone out of my pocket, scroll to the last text I got from Unknown, and type, "THANK YOU" and ten yellow heart emojis to the mysterious guide on the other side who helped me find my way this year. Whatever they were trying to do to help me worked big-time. But then.

Two seconds later, I hear a ding from right behind me. Weird. Then a new text pops up on my phone that says, "You're welcome, Ginge."

Wha . . . ?

I turn around, and boom. Finally, I come face-to-face with Unknown. And I'm not even surprised by who I see because it's who I should have known it was all along.

CHAPTER THIRTY

"Thank you, Mom," I say, and we hug for what feels like forever. Everything makes sense now. She *was* paying attention all along, even when it didn't seem like she was. Even when it seemed that all she cared about was her blog and the competitive crystal industry. But that's what moms do, I guess. They see everything.

"But just tell me one thing, woman. Was any of this because of the goddess ritual with the candle? Because if it was, I have to take back a lot of things I've said over the years and also probably take up yoga."

"Nope." She laughs. "It wasn't because of that. Even the chanting was just old 70s songs that your dad plays with his band. But you don't need magic when you have Google skills and good Wi-Fi, and a desire to help your kid figure out how awesome she is. Now bring Daisy over here because I have something else to tell you both."

By now, almost everyone has left the party, so it's easy to find Daisy chomping on potato chips at the snack table. She's *still* smiling from ear to ear, and I don't know if she'll ever stop. We might need to take her to the doctor.

"Hey, bestie!" she says when I walk up. "I had so much fun today. I'm exhausted!"

"Same here!" I say. "What will ever top this day? Even if I someday adopt a dog named Bruce, who water skis, which would be—"

"Awesome!" we say together then high-five each other.

How could I have even *thought* about going to Los Angeles today? Who needs a TV studio full of strangers when I have a garage full of friends?

The two of us walk over to where my parents are sitting together, holding hands and looking happy. I like it when they look like that.

"We just had a phone call about you girls," my mom says when she sees us. "And we need to talk about it."

Daisy and I look at each other in confusion. Did we do something wrong? We've been here the entire day, so that seems unlikely. We have an alibi! We didn't go on a crime spree! And the call couldn't be from Daisy's dad, either, because he's still here, relaxing in a lawn chair.

"The call was from the Kimmel people again," my mom continues. "I told them yesterday that you weren't doing the show today because your friend, and creative director, Daisy's party was more important to you."

"THE JIMMY KIMMEL SHOW!" Daisy yelps. "You turned down the show for my party?"

I shrug. Daisy gives me a tight bear hug, just like

her dad did earlier.

My mom continues, "The producers thought that was so amazing and charming that they're sending a crew here to Austin tomorrow to tape a segment for their show called FRIENDS ARE BENEFITS. Starring you two! You're both going to be on TV! And they said Chance can be an assistant producer for the day, too, because he did such a great job helping you with the videos. Can you believe it?"

Daisy and I turn to each other and smile.

We can.

Because friends are the most important thing in life.

And there's nothing funny about that.

AUTHOR'S NOTE

I get asked often if I was funny as a kid. And my answer is, "not really." In fact, I was more like Aanya, shy and quiet. (Although I didn't dress up like a unicorn!) I was goofy with my friends, and I liked reading books that made me laugh, but I wasn't the class clown. And I never wanted to be on stage like Ginger because I'm not that brave.

Luckily, I discovered that you can be funny on paper, too.

There are many different formats for writing humor. Parody, satire, knock-knock jokes, puns, sketches. And so many types of humor: dark, ironic, farcical, scatological (not mine or Ginger's favorite), silly, self-deprecating, etc. You'll most likely lean toward the style that makes you laugh the most.

And if you like writing humor, you can write funny books, TV shows, videos, billboards, movies, comic books, songs — the list goes on and on. The important thing is to just try it! Once you get a funny thought in your head, think about the best way to express it. In the kid comedy writing camp I teach every summer, we've written parodies of Katy Perry songs, ads for doughnuts, and a lot of jokes about cats. And here's the most important part: if it makes you laugh, then it's good.

Here's the second most important part: if it makes someone else sad, it's not good. Remember how Ginger "punched down and not up" in the talent show? That means she made fun of people for things they can't change. The rule to follow is "punch up, not down," where you poke fun at people in power. Like the president or the fancy rich guy. (But not your parents if you want them to keep buying you funny books like this one.)

What I love the most about humor, besides how fun it is, is that it can help us deal with difficult times in our lives, and maybe make us feel a little less alone. Ginger used humor as a coping mechanism when she was sad or feeling lonely, and so do I, and so should you! Remember: Laughter is the best medicine.

Thanks for reading and laughing!

ACKNOWLEDGMENTS

Thank you to BookBar's Nicole Sullivan for loving this book idea from the beginning, and to my brilliant editor Heather Garbo whose enthusiasm made the process even more fun. Thank you to Carey Albertine and Saira Rao who asked me years ago if I had an idea for a middle-grade book, and I said, "I do! And it'll be funny!" Thank you to my parents, Sharon and Wayne Willson, to my husband Chris, and to my sons Sam and Jack, for always supporting my writing. And finally, thank you to everyone who's ever made me laugh via their jokes, or shows, or writing, or even their TikTok videos that I find myself watching at 3 a.m. when I should be sleeping. Laughter will save us all.

Wendi Aarons is an award-winning humorist, writer and author of the funny book for adults, *I'm Wearing Tunics Now* (2022).

She has written for *McSweeney's*, *The New Yorker Daily Shouts*, *US Weekly*, *BuzzFeed*, *Texas Monthly* and more. Wendi's blog was named "Funniest Parenting Blog" by Parents Magazine and she won the Iris Award for "Most Entertaining Writer." She also teaches comedy writing camps for kids, and you should totally sign up for one. Wendi lives in Austin, Texas, with her husband and two sons. This is her first middle grade book. Find Wendi online at www.gingermancino.com.